Between a Ridge and a Hard Place

Is it love? Or sabotage?

After a year of being ignored as a woman by her boss, Morgan steps up her game—and strips down. What better way than a miniskirt to capture her hardheaded boss's attention? The butt floss she can do without, but hey, if the ploy works...and it does, with spectacular results. Now if only she can keep him interested permanently.

Ridge can't believe it when the woman he's quietly lusted after for a year shows up dressed...or rather, undressed...to drop any man to his knees. Instead of worrying about winning a bid after losing the last two under strange circumstances, he whisks her to his place to demolish any notion she might have of changing her mind.

Then it becomes clear why his company is losing bids—there's a mole planted in their midst. Ridge suddenly has to question Morgan's sudden transformation from faithful P.A. to office vixen.

Is she the woman he's been waiting for? Or a corporate saboteur sent to take him down?

Warning: Contains several graphic love scenes. You know, on the bed, on the couch...whichever is closest at the time.

Bridging the Gap

The higher she climbs, the harder he falls...

Carter Malone is usually the first one to make tracks before a woman starts getting any ideas. Permanent relationships don't fit into his personal blueprint. Now, for the first time in his life, he's burning up the sheets with a woman who makes him think about something more permanent...like spending the night. But she's holding something back, something he can't quite pin down.

As a woman in a man's world, Ryan Cooper is used to wearing a target on her back—and hiding her vulnerabilities. She hasn't let anything, not even the ever-present threat of an epileptic seizure, stop her from working her butt off to get the foreman's job with her stepfather's construction company. Then she discovers the guy she's been dating—okay, having the hottest sex of her life with—is the architect who designed the building she'll be overseeing. The last thing she needs is anyone thinking she slept with Carter to get the job.

Or worse, feeling sorry for her.

Before the dust clears, things get a lot more complicated. The previous foreman's injury was no accident, and whoever caused it is taking aim—at the target on Ryan's back.

Warning: This book contains almost fully clothed sex with a little bit o' spanking on an OCD-clean desk inside a construction trailer, a rogue set of pencils that just won't take stay for an answer, and sweet loving in a tub.

Maximum Temptation

Annmarie McKenna

Samhain Publishing, Ltd.
577 Mulberry Street, Suite 1520
Macon, GA 31201
www.samhainpublishing.com

Maximum Temptation
Print ISBN: 978-1-60928-069-7
Between a Ridge and a Hard Place Copyright © 2011 by Annmarie
McKenna
Bridging the Gap Copyright © 2011 by Annmarie McKenna
To the Max Copyright © 2011 by Annmarie McKenna

Editing by Sasha Knight

Between a Ridge and a Hard Place, ISBN 978-1-60504-032-5
First Samhain Publishing, Ltd. electronic publication: June 2008
Bridging the Gap, ISBN 978-1-60504-723-2
First Samhain Publishing, Ltd. electronic publication: August 2009
To the Max, ISBN 978-1-60928-030-7
First Samhain Publishing, Ltd. electronic publication: May 2010
First Samhain Publishing, Ltd. print publication: April 2011

Contents

Between a Ridge and a Hard Place

~9~

Bridging the Gap

~67~

To the Max

~139~

Between a Ridge and a Hard Place

Dedication

To the Playground for helping me get back on track. ☺
Thanks!

Chapter One

"How sweet. Little Morgan thinks she has a chance in hell of getting Ridge's attention. You know those clothes won't make a damn bit of difference, don't you?"

Morgan Crenshaw clenched her jaw. It was all she could do not to slap the smug look off Amy Lee's face.

"He doesn't go for ho," Amy Lee continued.

Oh, that was rich coming from someone who wasn't dressed much different. Amy Lee had gone too far. Yes, the skirt was mini and the top, well, she'd call it formfitting, but she did not look like a ho. Did she?

Amy Lee gave a contemptuous sniff as if she were better than everyone and flipped her long hair off her shoulder with the backs of her fingers. Morgan started to rise only to stop dead when her boss's business partner, Carter, crossed between her desk and Amy Lee, saving the other woman from Morgan's desire to strangle her.

"Sweet, Morg." Carter paused at her desk and took in her outfit. "Like the new duds. You get hit by the make-over fairy last night?"

"Something like that," she muttered and slumped back in her chair. Amy Lee's snort nearly had her getting back up.

"Bitch," she said to Amy Lee's retreating back.

A few seconds later the outer office was empty. The prissy woman who thought she was God's gift to men had finally gone back to her own workstation and Carter—one of the owners of the architectural firm, Malone and Casey, where she worked as the other owner's PA—had sequestered himself in his office.

She had to get to the task at hand and not let Amy Lee get the better of her. Today was announcement day for a bid they'd put in for the design of the Honor Center and there was plenty to do for when they won it. She was sure they would. Losing those last two bids had to have been a fluke, even in this uber-competitive business.

Morgan took a moment to collect herself, sucked in a deep breath and tried to clear away the ugliness that was Amy Lee. As if she wasn't already self-conscious enough about the outfit. Her sweaty palms itched. She wiped them on the short, *short* skirt she wouldn't normally be caught dead in. Jeans and a T-shirt were more her style, but since her tomboyish clothes hadn't caught the attention of a certain hardheaded man, she'd had to branch out.

She wiggled in her seat, shut her eyes and inhaled again. How the hell did women wear this kind of underwear? She smiled. Maybe *this* was why Amy Lee always looked like she had a stick up her ass. Only it wasn't a stick, it was a string one had to dig for in the crack of one's ass to get out. She must wear this kind of underwear all the time. In the hour since Morgan had arrived, she'd spent more time trying to pick the floss from between her cheeks than actually working. But hey, if Ridge Casey liked the black lacy string, who was she to care, right? Certainly enough women had paraded through the office dressed as she was now, so this had to be where his tastes ran. Morgan wasn't naïve. She knew where those skanky women ended up.

And there it was. She had turned into a skank. No better than the women who oohed and aahed and fawned over her boss like they had nothing better to do than drool over the most beautiful man in the world.

God, she was such a loser. Deflated, Morgan sank back

an jumped with a squeak and looked ready to bolt.
ous green eyes—now those he had noticed *many* times
re wide disks on her petite face. Big enough to drown
His erection jumped and he cursed under his breath
ook a step back.

shed a lock of hair behind her ear and looked
ut at him. Better get to the bottom of this now
d ravish her on his grandfather's desk, OPEN sign
d door, or not.

, what's going on, sweetheart?"

ach fluttered with his use of the endearment. He'd
ne before. At least, not with her. Now those sluts
rading through here...

fted her chin. "What do you mean?"

d a finger in her direction. "The um, er... Why are
e that?" he blurted, obviously trying hard not to

d its way across her skin. The mighty Ridge
tered. She had done that to him. Well, her and
outfit. She was freezing. Goose bumps pebbled
r nipples stood at attention beneath the cotton
uick glance down confirmed it. Crap. In a self-
she couldn't prevent, Morgan crossed her arms
he motion drew Ridge's gaze to her belly. The
as bare between the minimal amount of cloth
nd bottom. She swept one arm down to cover

s raspy voice had her looking up. One of his
a pen on the desktop, the other rested
n the region of his lap.

her pussy. She'd never seen that particular
t directed at her anyway.

into her chair. Her face flamed with both embarrassment for having lowered herself this far and anger for not having the nerve to flat-out go for the man of her dreams in her normal modus operandi. Maybe she should just go home and change before he saw her. If he didn't think she was good enough for him as is, she should move on.

"Morning, Morgan."

"Morning," she grunted, then shot up in her seat, her once heated cheeks draining of blood, leaving her lightheaded. Lord, she hadn't even seen him come in.

Ridge came to a dead stop at the door to his office, those fantastic navy blue eyes facing away from her, his hand resting on the knob.

Don't turn around. Don't turn around.

He cleared his throat. "Morgan?" His voice cracked despite how he'd tried to avoid it, but he didn't turn.

His broad shoulders were rigid beneath the starched white shirt that tapered down to lean hips. His ass clenched under his slacks. Morgan did a double take. *His ass clenched?* Had to be her imagination. She openly gawked—he *was* facing away from her, after all. There! He did it again. This time she didn't miss the action. No doubt his jaw was making the same movement. The man had a tic in his jaw whenever he was angry.

"Morgan," he said with more force, snapping her out of her perusal of his very fine backside.

"Yes, sir?"

His shoulders relaxed, as did his butt. Damn. He nodded once. "Just making sure it was you." Why did he sound so strangled?

Oh that's just great. She'd worn the dang clothes for nothing. Ridge opened the door to his inner office and stepped through, having yet to meet her gaze. Stare. She'd been staring, no question. He paused again and she thought this time he would face her, but after a slight hesitation and a shake of his head, he continued on. Perhaps her boss had been more affected by her virtual state of undress than he was prepared to be.

The corners of her mouth lifted. Maybe today would be her day after all.

Holy shit.

What the hell had happened to his PA? Taking a seat behind the huge mahogany desk that had been his grandfather's, he leaned a few inches to the left until he could see out the door to make sure he hadn't been dreaming.

Holy shit.

Nope. He'd seen right. His tomboy PA wasn't a tomboy anymore. She was all woman, and his cock agreed, coming to life to tent his slacks. Thank God he didn't have any clients this morning. In fact, if he could make it to the front door and turn the OPEN sign to CLOSED, he could make fine use of his massive erection. Too bad shutting out the public wouldn't keep the rest of the employees at bay. Hell, he needn't go any further than his own door to do that. All he had to do was bring her in his office, lock the door and—

Stop. Stop right there. This is your PA, for God's sake. He didn't date employees. Or fuck them on his desk with that glorious chestnut hair spread out across his memos, her legs wrapped around his waist while he plunged in and out of her sopping...

Holy shit.

Ridge shook his head to clear it. He didn't need this. It was hard enough to keep his mind from wandering to the woman just outside his door. The one he spent more time with and knew more about than any other woman in the world besides his sister and mother. The only one he really *wanted* to know more about.

Maybe she had a twin. Had to. N
she'd sent the identical twin she'd
her place so she wouldn't have to ta
his sensible, blend-into-the-crowd
work dressed the way she was.
scandalous.

He had to see the whole thing

"Morgan, get in here," he ba
about this right now. Their rec
focused on. The bid they shoul
way their last two bids—whi
hands down—had gone, he w
he saw a winning result.

"Yes, sir."

The shy, nervous reply
never been afraid of him. T
was her boss, she was hi
more and she'd never sho
more about him than he d

Holy shit.

Long, long legs—hel
had to go so he could
often—balanced somev
stiletto, but high enoug

A miniskirt cover
barely. Ridge swallow
transformed woman
visible between the f
hem of her...tank
making his mouth
poking out, beggin

Holy—

"Goddammit.
that phrase in th

Morg
Her gorge
before—w
a man in.
when she

"Stop.
She p
anywhere
before he d
and unlock

"Morga

Her ston
never used o
she'd seen pa

Morgan li

He waggle
you dressed li
look at her.

Hope sizzl
Casey was flus
this ridiculous
her skin and h
of her shirt. A d
conscious move
over her chest.
one she knew w
on both her top
that area too.

"Stop." Ridge
hands crushed
somewhere below

Heat flooded
look on his face. N

into her chair. Her face flamed with both embarrassment for having lowered herself this far and anger for not having the nerve to flat-out go for the man of her dreams in her normal modus operandi. Maybe she should just go home and change before he saw her. If he didn't think she was good enough for him as is, she should move on.

"Morning, Morgan."

"Morning," she grunted, then shot up in her seat, her once heated cheeks draining of blood, leaving her lightheaded. Lord, she hadn't even seen him come in.

Ridge came to a dead stop at the door to his office, those fantastic navy blue eyes facing away from her, his hand resting on the knob.

Don't turn around. Don't turn around.

He cleared his throat. "Morgan?" His voice cracked despite how he'd tried to avoid it, but he didn't turn.

His broad shoulders were rigid beneath the starched white shirt that tapered down to lean hips. His ass clenched under his slacks. Morgan did a double take. *His ass clenched?* Had to be her imagination. She openly gawked—he *was* facing away from her, after all. There! He did it again. This time she didn't miss the action. No doubt his jaw was making the same movement. The man had a tic in his jaw whenever he was angry.

"Morgan," he said with more force, snapping her out of her perusal of his very fine backside.

"Yes, sir?"

His shoulders relaxed, as did his butt. Damn. He nodded once. "Just making sure it was you." Why did he sound so strangled?

Oh that's just great. She'd worn the dang clothes for nothing. Ridge opened the door to his inner office and stepped through, having yet to meet her gaze. Stare. She'd been staring, no question. He paused again and she thought this time he would face her, but after a slight hesitation and a shake of his head, he continued on. Perhaps her boss had been more affected by her virtual state of undress than he was prepared to be.

The corners of her mouth lifted. Maybe today would be her day after all.

Holy shit.

What the hell had happened to his PA? Taking a seat behind the huge mahogany desk that had been his grandfather's, he leaned a few inches to the left until he could see out the door to make sure he hadn't been dreaming.

Holy shit.

Nope. He'd seen right. His tomboy PA wasn't a tomboy anymore. She was all woman, and his cock agreed, coming to life to tent his slacks. Thank God he didn't have any clients this morning. In fact, if he could make it to the front door and turn the OPEN sign to CLOSED, he could make fine use of his massive erection. Too bad shutting out the public wouldn't keep the rest of the employees at bay. Hell, he needn't go any further than his own door to do that. All he had to do was bring her in his office, lock the door and—

Stop. Stop right there. This is your PA, for God's sake. He didn't date employees. Or fuck them on his desk with that glorious chestnut hair spread out across his memos, her legs wrapped around his waist while he plunged in and out of her sopping...

Holy shit.

Ridge shook his head to clear it. He didn't need this. It was hard enough to keep his mind from wandering to the woman just outside his door. The one he spent more time with and knew more about than any other woman in the world besides his sister and mother. The only one he really *wanted* to know more about.

Maybe she had a twin. Had to. Maybe Morgan was sick and she'd sent the identical twin she'd only met last night to take her place so she wouldn't have to take a sick day. No way would his sensible, blend-into-the-crowd Morgan ever show up at work dressed the way she was. It was inappropriate. It was scandalous.

He had to see the whole thing.

"Morgan, get in here," he barked. He should not be thinking about this right now. Their recent bid was what he should be focused on. The bid they should win hands down. But given the way their last two bids—which should have also been won hands down—had gone, he wouldn't take an easy breath until he saw a winning result.

"Yes, sir."

The shy, nervous reply made him lower his brows. She'd never been afraid of him. They had an easy companionship. He was her boss, she was his assistant, even though he wanted more and she'd never shown any interest. Hell, Morgan knew more about him than he did.

Holy shit.

Long, long legs—hell, those fucking pants she always wore had to go so he could see those beautiful legs of hers more often—balanced somewhat precariously on high heels. Not stiletto, but high enough, which made her legs look even longer.

A miniskirt covered the tops of her thighs. Barely. Just barely. Ridge swallowed and continued his open study of the transformed woman before him. A strip of tanned belly was visible between the fabric someone had deemed a skirt and the hem of her...tank top? Her small breasts strained the top, making his mouth water. He could even see her beaded nipples poking out, begging for him to take them in his mouth.

Holy—

"Goddammit." How many times had he mentally repeated that phrase in the last few minutes?

Morgan jumped with a squeak and looked ready to bolt. Her gorgeous green eyes—now those he had noticed *many* times before—were wide disks on her petite face. Big enough to drown a man in. His erection jumped and he cursed under his breath when she took a step back.

"Stop."

She pushed a lock of hair behind her ear and looked anywhere but at him. Better get to the bottom of this now before he did ravish her on his grandfather's desk, OPEN sign and unlocked door, or not.

"Morgan, what's going on, sweetheart?"

Her stomach fluttered with his use of the endearment. He'd never used one before. At least, not with her. Now those sluts she'd seen parading through here...

Morgan lifted her chin. "What do you mean?"

He waggled a finger in her direction. "The um, er... Why are you dressed like that?" he blurted, obviously trying hard not to look at her.

Hope sizzled its way across her skin. The mighty Ridge Casey was flustered. She had done that to him. Well, her and this ridiculous outfit. She was freezing. Goose bumps pebbled her skin and her nipples stood at attention beneath the cotton of her shirt. A quick glance down confirmed it. Crap. In a self-conscious move she couldn't prevent, Morgan crossed her arms over her chest. The motion drew Ridge's gaze to her belly. The one she knew was bare between the minimal amount of cloth on both her top and bottom. She swept one arm down to cover that area too.

"Stop." Ridge's raspy voice had her looking up. One of his hands crushed a pen on the desktop, the other rested somewhere below in the region of his lap.

Heat flooded her pussy. She'd never seen that particular look on his face. Not directed at her anyway.

Time to adopt a bold new attitude. If ever she was going to get the man to notice her, this was it.

She unfolded her arms, rested her hands on her hips and shifted her weight to one foot.

"Stop what, exactly?" Okay, so trying for a sultry voice didn't sound quite as good out loud as it did in her head.

"Moving," he murmured, his gaze zeroing in on her breasts. He wouldn't find much. A sorry B cup was about all she had to offer. Hell, B was fudging just a bit. They were more like an A plus. If only an A plus meant for your boobs what it meant in school, she'd be all set.

But he kept looking, his mouth open and his nostrils flaring softly.

Snap. The pen in his hand broke in two pieces. Ink bled onto his skin and dripped on his paperwork.

"Shit." Ridge jerked out of his appraisal of her body and stamped at the mess with a tissue. By the time he'd gotten the worst up, both hands were sticky with black ink. Glaring down at them, he growled with sheer menace. Six long strides took him around his desk to the private bathroom in his office. As he brushed by her she thought she heard him mutter, "This is going to be a long day."

Morgan giggled. Served him right for ogling her breasts.

Wait. That's what she wanted. She waited patiently, as patiently as she could under the circumstances, for him to finish cleaning up. When he finally returned and faced her once more, he busied himself with trying to dry his stained hands. Soap hadn't taken care of the problem. She should apologize, but it hadn't been her fault. If he couldn't control his reactions, he ought to at least be more careful. She pursed her lips and fought the urge to whistle as if not noticing his state of unease.

"Why the hell are you dressed like that?" *Why are you messing with my head?*

Damn ink. He'd never get it off. He swiped at it uselessly with the paper towel, careful not to transfer the shit to his clothes. Clothes, or lack thereof in Morgan's case, were the cause of this mess. Damn *her* for standing in front of him in a way he'd never seen her before, begging him for something he couldn't give her at this particular second. Jesus, all the blood in his body had flowed straight to his groin.

His normally cool assistant pursed her lips. She thought this was funny. Ridge wondered how funny she would find the situation if he threw her down on the butter-soft leather couch across the room and ripped those threads off her pretty little, very sexy, made-to-be-touched-by-a-man's-hands body.

She looked down at herself as if just now noticing her state of undress. Morgan was completely out of her comfort zone. He'd wage his entire company on it.

"What's wrong with what I'm wearing?"

Ridge snorted. "Not a goddamn thing." *If you were dancing on a pole right now.* He skirted by her, half afraid if he touched her he'd be inside her in less time than it took to lay her down.

Fuck laying her down, he'd take her standing up. "I'm just not used to you wearing them," he admitted.

"Well…"

When she hesitated, he met her gaze. She nibbled on her lip, and he groaned and dropped his chin to his chest. The little minx had no idea the havoc she was playing on him. Or maybe she did…

"Well what?" he said a tad too forceful.

Morgan caught her breath and stood straighter. He had to give her credit. She lifted her head and looked him square in the eye. "Every girl has the right to feel like a girl sometimes."

Was that what this was all about? Her testing out her feminine side? "All right." He sat back down, trying to decide what he could salvage from the ink disaster. "Just wish the skirt wasn't quite so short," he murmured.

"What was that?"

He glanced up at her. "Hmm?"

Now she looked exasperated. *Welcome to my world, sweetheart.*

"You don't like it?"

"Oh, me likey." Damn. He hadn't meant to say that out loud.

"Really?"

Great. Now he had her preening. "You'll have every man coming in the door distracted." And all the other male employees too. Shit. The mere thought had him turning green. He didn't want any other man seeing what he considered his.

What the hell? His? Where had that thought come from? He'd been attracted to her from day one but she hadn't reciprocated the interest so he'd let her be. There'd been no reason to distract from their easy working relationship.

He had to get her out of here now and dressed more, well, more...dressed. In sweats if need be. In his sweats. After a long romp between the sheets of his bed and another round in the shower. And perhaps a second go-round in the bed. Until they were both completely sated and ready to sleep for twelve hours. Then he would stuff her delectable body in his old workout sweats and keep her tucked away from the lewd eyes of all men everywhere.

He jumped from the chair, stormed around the desk and grabbed Morgan's elbow, leading her from the office. He wasn't going to get a damn thing done in his present state of mind. Carter would have to take over for the time being.

"Let's go," he snarled.

Another mouse-like squeak erupted from her lips as she was dragged away. Amy Lee, who'd appeared back at Morgan's desk, no doubt to continue taunting her, wrenched her head and audibly gasped as they rushed by. Morgan didn't even have the chance to gloat. Her clothes may not have turned Ridge on but they'd certainly gotten his notice.

"Where are we going?" In the ridiculous heels, she stumbled over the threshold and out onto the sidewalk. Ridge twisted in time to catch her against his hard chest, knocking the wind from her lungs. She had to grab something to balance herself, and the only thing handy was his shirt.

"You okay?"

Staring at where her hands had landed—right on top of his incredible pecs—and unable to speak past the sudden rush of drool on her tongue, she nodded. Now was her chance. If she stood on her tiptoes and tilted her head just right and opened her mouth...

His arm burnt a path along the small of her back, crushing her to him, making the ridge of hardness at her abdomen very evident.

Her eyes widened. He had a hard-on. For her! Amy Lee was so going down.

"Can you walk now?" His chest vibrated beneath her fists.

His lips were perfect, his breath minty. The woodsy, manly aftershave he wore tickled her nose and his pulse thrummed at the base of his throat. She itched to lean in and sniff him right there, maybe give it a little lick before working her way up—

He lifted her gaze to his with a thumb under her chin. "I said, are you okay to walk?" The rumble was back, this time against her hardened nipples since he had her whole body squashed to his.

"Uh-huh." She licked her lips and fought to keep her eyes open when a tingle of heat slid through her belly and sizzled between her legs.

With a sharp nod, he grabbed her hand and started dragging again. Keeping up with him in the unfamiliar shoes was proving impossible. She stopped short, yanking him back since he still had a hold of her hand. A look of surprise crossed his face as she tore off the offensive heels.

Letting out a big breath, Morgan smiled. "Much better." She tried for cool and confident—absurd really, when she was standing on the sidewalk half-dressed and barefoot, being pulled by her gorgeous boss to who knew where. She didn't even want to imagine the attention the two of them were most likely drawing.

A quick peek revealed several people around them. A few curious as to her behavior, most others lost in their own world.

"Now?"

"What?" She jerked her gaze back to Ridge to find him staring at her feet. Wiggling her toes, she muttered, "Sorry. These things were killing me."

Ridge grunted then brought his steady regard of her feet up her legs and abdomen—pausing at her A plus breasts—until he reached her face. Her tummy flipped with the fire she saw glaring from his eyes. There was a predatory hunger in them that made her think he wanted to devour her whole. A sudden flutter of apprehension flitted through her system. She'd wanted him for so long, had dressed the way she had today with the full intention of garnering his attention, but now that she had it, Morgan wasn't one hundred percent positive she was ready for it.

Never had any man made her feel the way she did at this very second. Like her miniscule panties were going to combust if he didn't rip them off her and have his wicked way with her body.

"You were saying?" she finally rasped, perfectly willing to let him drag her off anywhere he wanted to.

"What I want to do to you doesn't require saying anything."

Chapter Two

Her mouth opened and closed like a fish. Good. He'd taken her by surprise. Not nearly as well as she had him, but he had to start somewhere.

A shrill catcall came from the construction site across the street. No doubt one of the idiots on the roof thought Ridge had picked himself up a hooker. He ought to head over there and blacken the pissant's eye. But that would take too long.

"Come on." He tugged her again and headed for his Tahoe. At least the tinted windows would provide some privacy. Not enough for the thoughts running straight from his brain to his cock, but some.

"You still haven't told me where we're going. Do you have some last-minute meeting or something?"

Ridge snorted. If she thought for one second he would take her to a meeting with any of the clients they normally met with dressed this way, she was on crack. The thought had him stopping in his tracks. He lifted his head to feel the sun's warmth on his cheeks. Surely not... No. Not possible. He'd never seen his PA drink even the smallest dribble of alcohol, let alone smoke a cigarette. No way would she do something decidedly more damaging to the body he'd finally discovered was absolutely fabulous.

The one he wanted to get his hands on. Now. After he got her out of the clothes everyone out here could see her in.

"Home," he growled.

"Why?"

He didn't answer until they'd reached his SUV and he trapped her between the passenger door and his body. He'd had enough with roaming eyes on his woman.

Ah, Christ. He'd done it again. She wasn't his woman. But dammit, she would be in a short time if he had anything to say about it.

Ridge clenched his jaw and hissed out a breath when she struggled to get her hands free from where they were trapped between their bodies. Her knuckles caressed the hard length of his erection, and he nearly begged her to take him out and do a better job.

"The clothes, woman."

Her look down was hampered by his body. "And what exactly is wrong with my clothes?"

"Hm. Don't even try to play coy with me. That outfit would stop a bullet train on a dime."

Her lips pursed. Knowing the girl inside the revealing top and skirt, Ridge had to wonder again at why she'd gone to such lengths.

"Who's it for, sweetheart?" The question ripped from his heart. If she said another man's name...

Those emerald eyes sought his, and for a moment his breath caught. He knew what he wanted her answer to be, but what if, just what if it wasn't all for him?

"You." The simple word whispered against his lips. He hadn't realized he'd moved closer, but he took the advantage and pressed his mouth to hers, swallowing her whimper.

Her hands found their way around his neck, keeping him immobile, right where he wanted to be. Morgan moaned and opened for him, allowing him access to the warm recesses of her mouth. She tasted of her habitual morning Coke and something else sweet and sugary. Her tentative tongue stroked his, first shyly then with more force. Ridge tilted her head one way and angled his the other to deepen their kiss. It wasn't good enough.

A honking horn coupled with a crude shout of, "Get her, buddy!" snapped his attention back into place. Breathing hard, Ridge eased back and stroked Morgan's cheeks with his thumbs.

For a few heartbeats, a dazed look took over the features of her face. Her tongue darted out to lick along her swollen, well-kissed lips, making Ridge groan.

"Wow." She had to clear her throat, and he didn't know whether to be offended or proud he'd put her in such a state.

After a stab of the unlock button on his remote, he reached behind her, opened the door and eased her into the seat. He had her legs swung inside and the seat belt buckled before she knew what hit her. He slammed the door shut, finalizing her entrapment, and took a look back at the architect business he and his best friend Carter had started ten years ago.

Despite his anxiety over the bidding war, Malone and Casey would have to deal without Ridge and Morgan this afternoon.

Several minutes passed before Morgan's wits came back. She felt scrambled. Ridge Casey had just thoroughly demolished her with a kiss in front of the entire town. She barely refrained from pumping her fist in the air and had to keep her focus out the window so her boss wouldn't see the huge grin on her face.

It dimmed the more she thought about things. Had he only done this because of the clothes? She sure as shit wasn't going to make a habit of wearing this type of outfit. The piece of floss was still up her crack. It was the most freaking uncomfortable thing God had ever allowed to be created.

She squirmed in the soft leather seat, which only caused the strand to work itself deeper.

"Stop wiggling." Ridge's continual growling this morning

made her smile. She'd never seen the man so flustered. It wouldn't make her dress up tomorrow, but still. If he didn't want the real woman, then he didn't deserve her anyway. This superficial Morgan had done her job and gotten through his thick skull. Now she had to find a way to keep him interested in the normal her and keep her heart intact.

"I will as soon as I can get out of this ridiculous piece of underwear."

"Excuse me?" Both of his eyebrows shot upward.

"Did I just say that out loud?" Stupid, stupid woman. Open mouth, insert foot.

"You did. Now tell me what you meant."

"Nothing." Jesus. She might as well dye her hair blonde for the way she was acting today. The damned outfit was making her act like a complete fool.

"Not nothing. I want to know. The whole thing sounds very intriguing."

Sarcastic bastard.

"I'm waiting." The tone of his voice was akin to him tapping his foot while he waited.

"Then I hope you're comfortable."

His hand landed on her thigh just above her knee. Her breath hitched in her throat at the sight of his tanned hand on her slightly paler thigh. More so when his fingertips squeezed and his thumb swiped back and forth.

"I will be soon." The smooth tone of his promise made her shiver. "Now tell me, sweetheart."

Damn. When would she learn to keep her big mouth shut? His palm slid further up her leg until his pinky and ring finger disappeared beneath the edge of her skirt. Her tongue felt like cotton and her throat parched. She forced herself to relax. This closeness was what she wanted, right?

"The longer it takes you to talk, the closer I get to finding out what you meant on my own, Morgan."

She yelped and staved off his further advancement with both hands on his. The man had never touched her in all the time she'd worked for him, outside of a hand on her back when ushering her through a door or an incidental passing of fingertips, and suddenly he was inches away from her core and the clit throbbing there.

"Stupid thong, okay?" she hissed.

A smile split his lips and his hand retreated to the place above her knee as he turned into an obviously affluent neighborhood.

"I thought you were taking me home."

Ridge turned to her. "I am."

"But this isn't where I..." Of course it wasn't. He didn't know where she lived. Which only left one reasonable conclusion.

"How, exactly, is it you want me to change at your house?" she asked, turning the conversation.

He snorted and that little place called her womb clenched with a scared thrill. She'd been to bed with a man before, a few even, but none of them could hold a candle to Ridge. There was a certain magnetism about him, a strong connection she felt to him, while he probably only saw her as another notch on his bedpost.

Man, her morals had really sunk low.

Or maybe his sister, or one of his old conquests, had left clothes at his house, and since he lived much closer, he thought they'd just pop on over and grab some.

Great. She nibbled her lip. Now she wasn't sure what his motivations were.

Right. That's why he had his hand up your skirt a minute ago.

"Who said anything about changing?" His fingers tightened on her leg. At least one of them seemed sure of what might happen in the very near future.

Morgan swallowed and pressed her knees together. Surely the seat beneath her was getting wet. She couldn't remember a man ever making her cream herself by his mere presence alone, yet Ridge did so on a daily basis. She really was a shallow, shallow woman.

A shallow woman who was finally getting the chance to sleep with her boss.

Chapter Three

Ridge pulled into his driveway and cut the engine halfway up. He was out of the Tahoe and around to her door before she could think about what was happening and change her mind. She obviously had his seduction in mind this morning or they wouldn't be where they were right now.

His cock practically drummed against his zipper. If he didn't get her inside, or rather inside *her* soon, the damn thing was going to bust out.

But first. "Please tell me you're thinking along the same lines here, sweetheart." He leaned close and inhaled her sweet vanilla scent, nuzzling her neck and planting a row of kisses along the smooth column.

"Uh-huh."

Good. She was just as affected.

"I've been trying to stay away from you, Morgan, trying to keep us from this position, but when I saw you dressed like this when I walked in, I nearly lost it. I can't stay away anymore."

Her throat moved when she swallowed and her face turned to his, her lips brushing his. She started the kiss, but he took control, licking along the seam of her mouth until she let him in. They melded together, but not nearly close enough. Ridge reached across her body, unbuckled her seat belt and swung her into his arms, capturing her moan of protest with deeper penetration of his tongue.

Savoring her weight in his arms and the feel of her body flush against his, he carried her to the front door. To open it he had to prop her along the jamb. The alarm beeped inside. Keeping a hand on Morgan, he pulled her through, punched the code to disarm the system then pressed her back to the wall so he could continue to devour her.

"What was that you were saying about not staying away?" she rasped, panting.

"Not going to." Ridge lifted her into his arms again and climbed the stairs.

"Good grief, put me down."

"No way. Can't let you get away."

She laid her hand on his cheek. "I'm not going anywhere," she said softly.

"Damn straight." Thank God he'd kind of cleaned up this morning, otherwise Morgan would have gotten an eyeful of his tendency towards being the ultimate bachelor—i.e. leaving his clothes heaped on the chair and his towel on the bathroom floor. He hadn't made the bed, but then they were just about to destroy it anyway. He finally set her feet on the floor and caught her when she swayed.

"Now I've got you where I want you."

"Oh yeah?"

"Definitely." He trailed a finger from her chin, down between her breasts, to her bellybutton that peeked out from beneath her ridden-up tank.

"So...you think you're capable of making—er, umm...*fucking*," she blurted, "while standing up?"

He smiled at her stumble over the word. "Perfectly, but there won't be any fucking going on."

Morgan's eyes widened. "But...I thought...that we—"

He nodded and put a finger of his free hand over her lips to silence her. "Sweetheart, what we're about to do is more than fucking." He moved the hand on her belly back up, pulling the hem of her shirt up with it, revealing her skin inch by inch.

"It is?"

"Mm-hmm. Lift your arms."

After a second's hesitation and a nibble on her lower lip she did, allowing him to strip the thin material up and off.

If his cock wasn't already as hard as possible, it would have gotten that way at the sight greeting him. Perfect firm breasts, just enough to fill his palms.

"They're small." Morgan crossed her arms over her chest.

Ridge took her wrists and drew them away before covering what she found as an imperfection. "They're perfect." Her nipples were drawn taut and she shivered when he rasped his thumbs across them. "They're mine." Unable to resist, he lowered his head and wrapped his lips around one of the dusky pink tips.

She moaned and arched into him. He tweaked the other nipple with his fingers, tugging on it until she gasped. Her body lifted onto her toes.

"Oh, God."

"God's not here, sweetheart, just me."

"'S'nough. Don't need him. Need you." Her mouth found his again, and her hands wound around his head to link at the back of his neck.

"I'm all yours." He walked her backward to the bed and carefully laid her down. She stretched languorously, a tiny smile on her lips as he perused her body. "These have to go." He hooked his fingers in the waistband of the skirt and pulled it and the nonexistent panties off in one swipe.

Morgan's shyness returned full force. Her right knee started to rise and Ridge knew she was about to cross her legs.

"Uh-uh. No hiding, remember?" He knelt on the floor between her knees and ran his palms up her thighs. The skin there was so soft and smooth. He kissed the path he'd made with his hands and zeroed in on the flesh at her apex, spreading her outer lips with his thumbs then gently blowing on the heat simmering there.

Her hands came down to cover herself. He snorted. "As if that will keep me out, Morg."

"Sorry."

"Hands above your head," he growled.

They went. Shakily, but they moved up. When she held her head up so she could see what he was doing, he caught her gaze and found a mixture of uncertainty and anticipation there.

"Here." He jumped to his feet and grabbed the pillow from the head of the bed, which he placed under her neck so she didn't strain herself. He planned on being there for awhile. "Better?"

Her tongue dashed out and she nodded.

"Are you gonna...ya know...take yours off?" She regarded his clothes up and down, pausing for a long moment at his groin. There was no mistaking what she saw tenting his pants.

"Oh yeah." Ridge attacked the belt, button and zipper of his trousers, toed his shoes off, and yanked both his pants and underwear off, then tossed them over his shoulder. Next came the tie, which he wrenched off, and then the top three buttons of the shirt. To hell with the rest—he stripped it off like a T-shirt over his head—and stood patiently while she took her fill of his nakedness.

Morgan felt her nostrils flare. The man was art personified. Perfection. Sculptured pecs, ribbed abs, muscular thighs, rigid cock standing at attention. Lord, he was big. For a second she panicked. She'd had sex before, a few times, but Ridge brought new meaning to being filled.

Her voice had long since left her. Still staring at his penis that now gleamed with a drop of pre-come, she suddenly had the urge to put her mouth to better use. She rose to her elbow, ready to put to action what her brain wanted. His hand stopped her.

"Not now." His words were a strangled laugh. "It'll be over before we start if you do that."

Damn. He'd read her intentions. He dropped to his knees again and spread her wide before she could even comment. Then his tongue licked her from back to front and she couldn't comment. It swirled, it danced, it stabbed. She threw her head back and fisted the comforter.

A thick finger entered her slowly and pulled back. In and out in a rhythm that wasn't enough. His tongue teased her clit, but it wasn't helping, only infuriating her. She reached for his head and grabbed hold of his hair.

"More," she demanded, seizing him by the ears and stabbing him with what she hoped was a get-your-tongue-in-gear sort of look. Enough playing with her. She was too wound up for games right now.

He smiled, disengaged her hand and went back to work.

Morgan groaned in frustration and resorted to begging. "Please, please, please, please." What she got was his cooler breath across her heated sheath.

"I'm savoring."

"Savor later," she hissed.

"Finally, the feisty Morgan I know and love."

Love? Had he really just said that? Whatever. She couldn't think about it now. Finally he went to work in earnest, lapping at her like there was no tomorrow. Two fingers filled her pussy at the same time as his tongue flicked back and forth over her clit, making her gasp. She lifted her hips in time with his penetration. Closer and closer...she exploded. The tingling took over her clit, her thighs clenched around his head, and her breathing labored in and out of her lungs.

Long seconds later she realized he now stood between her legs, a smug look of satisfaction on his face and a condom on his cock. Where he'd gotten it, she didn't know, didn't care.

"You're beautiful when you come."

His lips were shiny with her juices and she could see him in the broad daylight. She'd never had sex in the light before, had never clearly seen the look on her previous lovers' faces. Ridge's was in true predatory form right now. He bent, hooked his arms under her thighs and urged her bottom closer until it just hung off the edge of the bed.

Never taking his gaze off hers, he wrapped her legs around his waist, settled the head of his cock at her entrance and thrust home.

Morgan slammed her eyes shut at the sudden intrusion that verged within an inch of pain and left her breathless. When she opened her eyes again, she realized he hadn't moved. Instead, he stood above her, his jaw ticking, his eyes closed, his chin raised slightly as if he were basking in some hidden glory. She supposed he was. In *her* glory.

"Okay?" Ridge murmured.

"Yes." She wiggled her hips, wanting him to move. The orgasm he'd given her hadn't been enough apparently because her clit started to throb. She reached for it with her third finger only to have her hand swatted away.

"Mine." Sweat had beaded on his forehead and chest, and it seemed like it was taking a supreme effort on his part to stay still.

"Can you move...or something?"

"Not yet," he rasped. His thumb found her nub and pressed.

Morgan arched her hips, impaling his cock impossibly farther into her, and his breath hissed out.

Ridge withdrew and she immediately felt the loss. She crossed her ankles to tug him back.

"Woman," he grated between his teeth, pinning her with a threatening look. "I'm hanging on here by a thread, and I'd appreciate it if you would just give me a second."

A tiny smile lifted the corners of her mouth. "One." She shifted her hips again, sucking him back in.

Her reward was a stinging smack to her butt. She yelped.

"Don't play with me, sweetheart, or things are bound to get rough."

"I might like rough."

His eyes narrowed to dangerous slits. "I never knew."

"You do now."

He tortured her with a slow thrust forward and even longer drag out. Now a smile graced his lips. His fingertips dug into her hips, not hurting, but enough to tell her he was in control. Ridge bent over and latched onto one of her nipples, sucking it deep into his mouth and shoving his cock against her womb. The twin sensation had her bucking under him.

He let go of her nipple with a pop. "Damn it, woman, you're killing me."

"Like you're not killing me?" she cried.

With a lingering lick to the unattended breast, he rose up and fucked her. He'd said this wouldn't be fucking, but what else could you call the frenzied action of his hips as he pounded into her? Each drag of his cock in her pussy set her inner muscles to twitching. His thumb moved on her clit and she was a goner. This orgasm tore through her, leaving her screaming in its wake.

"Shit."

She barely heard his guttural shout through her own writhing. He slammed into her one last time and stiffened, squeezing her hips to keep her immobile as he spent himself inside her. Even through the barrier of latex, she felt his every pulse within her.

When the contractions finally quit, she glanced up to find a look of wonderment on Ridge's face. He collapsed beside her, making sure to brace his weight on his elbows, and buried his face in the crook of her neck and shoulder.

"We should have done that a long time ago," he mumbled against her neck.

"Uh-huh." She could hardly breathe, let alone talk at the moment. "Didn't know you wanted to."

"Oh I definitely wanted to. You're the one who never showed any interest."

Morgan reared her head back so she could look him. "Me? You're the one who didn't show interest."

"Only because I didn't think you did."

"Lord. Remember that day I interviewed? I could hardly look at you without drooling."

"So why didn't you say anything?"

"Because, you big dolt. You were about to become my boss and unlike certain other employees you have, I wasn't about to jeopardize my job by panting after you like a lovesick puppy."

His already re-hardening cock twitched inside her and for a second, Morgan lost her concentration. She bit her lip and closed her eyes, trying to hold onto the sensation of him moving deep within her.

"Did you just call me a dolt, sweetheart?" His quiet question fanned across her ear, making her shiver.

She swallowed. "I did."

His hips shifted forward, sparking off a tingling at her clit. "Which one of my employees pants after me?" Amusement rang loud and clear in his voice.

"Never mind."

Another press of his cock, and she bore down on him with a moan.

"Tell me," Ridge coaxed.

"No."

He withdrew and slid back in. "I can keep doing this all day." He nibbled at her ear.

"Damn you."

"Tell me what I want to know and I'll give you what you want."

"Amy Lee," she blurted, wrapping her arms around him and scoring his ass with her nails. His butt squeezed taut.

"You play dirty, baby." He flexed his hips, pushing into her with more force this time.

"Yessss."

Raising up and pulling out, he chuckled.

"Wha—?"

Ridge stripped the used condom and disposed of it in a tissue before tearing open a new one with his teeth and rolling it on. "I think you need to work for this one."

A sense of foreboding stole over Morgan. There was a definite gleam of enjoyment in his eyes. He crawled onto the bed and over her, deliberately dragging his penis across her torso and shoulder, to settle on his back near the center of the bed. He crossed his feet and propped his head on his hands.

"Come and get me," he beckoned.

Morgan rolled her eyes and sucked in her bottom lip. She couldn't help but be intrigued by the opportunity he presented. A chance to control the show? To determine how deep she took him and how fast? He didn't know what he was in for.

"Do your worst," he said, smiling, as if he'd read her mind.

What girl wouldn't take what was being offered here?

"How many women have you been with?"

His sudden raised eyebrow meant she'd shocked him. "You have to ask that now?"

She shrugged, joining him by straddling his abdomen, unself-conscious in the least when her juice slickened his flesh. His palms came to rest on her hips, then caressed up and down her sides.

"I just want to know if I'm anything more than a roll in the sack, a notch on your bedpost, a ship passing in the—"

He shushed her with a finger across her lips. "I get it."

"I'm just saying, it might be a little awkward to go to work every day after having slept with the boss." *Possessive much?* Her cheeks heated. How could she have said what she'd just said?

"More so for me, you little minx." He pinched her ass. "How can I work knowing this body is out there hiding in those baggy clothes you prefer?"

"I knew it," she crowed.

"Knew what?"

"That I'd only catch your eye by dressing like Amy...like a skank."

There went the eyebrow again. "Sweetheart, it wasn't the clothes that caught my eye. I mean, yeah, today they did, but you've been in my line of sight for a while. I was kinda hoping you'd get jealous from seeing all my...*friends*, and take a stand. Now, do you mind?" He nodded to where she sat, indicating he was ready for her to start.

Instead Morgan trailed a fingernail down his chest. "So you had all your lovers parade in front of me so I'd get jealous? That's kind of...eew."

"Lovers?" He cracked out a laugh. "Baby, I haven't had a lover since I hired you."

Her eyes widened and she sucked in a breath.

"Surprised?"

"But I thought..." She narrowed her eyes. "You go on plenty of dates."

"Yep. Dates. That's all they were. Dates. I did not sleep with any of them."

Now she snorted. "Must have pissed off quite a few women this year then."

"Is that how you see me? Like a stud service?"

"If the shoe fits."

"If the— I'll show you how something fits." He yanked her chest down to his and suddenly her world turned upside down. When she opened her eyes, it was to find that indeed it had. Ridge had reversed their positions and now hovered over her, his length between her legs, his cock poised at her entrance.

"The cock fits," he grunted and slid in to the hilt.

Morgan gasped as he raked against muscles unused to being used so thoroughly. "I thought I was supposed to be running the show this time."

"You took too long and talked too much. Had to take matters into my own hands." He bent and mouthed a nipple. "Whenever you're ready to accept what I've told you, then I'll let you take control. Until then, I guess I just have to show you how much you turn me on."

He pressed his advantage where it counted most. The breath strangled in her throat. Had to be his cock choking her, he was so deep inside her.

"One year, Morgan." His words were strained. "One year I've been waiting for any kind of sign from you. The least little bit of interest. When I showed up today and saw you dressed the way you were, I knew I couldn't let any other man see you that way." His cock worked lazily in and out of her. "And then when you said it was for me, you were a goner. Mine."

She needed more than his slow thrusts. Lifting her hips, she met him halfway. The angle forced her clit to his pelvis, where she ground herself against him, seeking the contact.

"You like that?" Ridge wrapped an arm beneath her ass and held her to him, then started thrusting. "Shit. I can't even think when I get this close to you. I wanted slow and easy, but my cock wants fast and hard."

"Ridge?"

"What?"

"Shut up and fuck me."

His smile lit up his face. "Yes, ma'am."

Carter turned, a grim look on his face. "I'm afraid so, Ridge."

"No."

Carter sat back in the seat and spread his hands. "Where is she?"

Ridge's breath caught. *Gone. She had something she had to... Shit.* Had she fucking played him? Had she panicked when he'd told her there was a mole at Malone and Casey? Is that what she had to do that was so all-fired important instead of coming back here with him? Had all the clothes and sex been a distraction for him?

"Son of a bitch." He didn't want to believe it. Couldn't believe it. Not from Morgan, his PA, the woman who'd been closer to him over the course of the last year than his own sister. He hadn't been lying to her when he'd told her he hadn't been with a woman since hiring her. Had *she* been lying to *him*?

"Where is she, Ridge?" Carter repeated.

Ridge dragged a hand through his hair and sank onto the corner of the desk. He shook his head. "No. No. She didn't do this, Car. You know she isn't capable of this."

"I wouldn't have thought so either, but damn it, Ridge, the evidence is all right here." Carter stabbed a finger at the computer screen.

"You know as well as I do that computers can be manipulated. It has to be a plant."

"Because you slept with her?"

Ridge stood, his fist cocked at his side.

Carter threw up his hands. "I'm just saying. She's been with you for a year, and now all of a sudden she wants to be your bed buddy? She's never shown a lick of interest in you until today. You want me to think this is a coincidence? Come on, Ridge, what else am I supposed to think when the woman's not even here to defend herself?"

The same goddamn thing I am. "Christ."

"Exactly. I think we've been played."

Fuck. Ridge wiped his face with both hands. If he couldn't go after Carter's pretty face, then the wall was looking pretty good to take out some of his anger on. "All right, let's think this out logically. We know how easy it is to plant evidence. Maybe it's someone else. Let's not jump the gun and automatically pin this on Morgan until we hear from her."

"Do you think we *will* hear from her?"

Ridge clamped down his jaw. If she didn't show up, he'd hunt her down himself. No. She didn't do it. He had faith in her.

Question was, did he have too much?

"She'll be back."

Carter eyed him suspiciously before nodding once. "Okay. I don't want to believe it's her either. So say she's being framed. Who has access to this computer?"

Ridge snorted. "Anyone. We're in the outer office. Literally anyone can come in off the street and sit down here."

Carter raised an eyebrow. "Kind of grasping at straws there, aren't you, Ridge? How likely do you think it is that someone would walk in here, packed with insider knowledge just to use against us?"

"Not likely," Ridge agreed, "but possible."

"You're right. But let's narrow it down to our employees." Carter checked off on his fingers. "Raymond, Susan, Olivia, Ted, Jack, Amy Lee, Martin, not to mention the cleaning crew."

"What could anyone from the cleaning crew actually gain from sabotaging an architectural business?"

"Money? I know you don't really need me to answer that."

Fine. He'd give him that. "What do we know about Biggs and Hilliard then? Like who works for them. Anyone we know, someone we pissed off and they're out to get us? I'm just trying to straighten things out before we go accusing the wrong person."

"And what if she's the right person, Ridge?"

Chapter Five

Morgan felt a zillion times more normal in regular clothes. She flicked away a piece of lint from the navy cotton shirt she'd donned and pushed through Malone and Casey's door to a hustle and bustle she wasn't used to. The head of the security firm they used, Max Jansen, stood like a sentinel next to her desk, his arms crossed over his chest. She could tell from his profile there was a serious look on his face.

She understood his seriousness. Someone selling information, someone she probably knew and worked with on a daily basis, was not a laughing matter. Max shifted his weight, revealing Carter at her computer, studying something. For a second she wondered why they were using her system. It seemed like the sort of the thing that might be better discussed somewhere private. And then it hit her. Of course they had to investigate everyone. It stung that she might be lumped in with the suspects, but then she supposed everyone in the office would be a suspect at first. What was it they said? Keep your friends close and your enemies closer? Something like that.

So based on Carter's expression was she a friend or an enemy? Better find out. She stepped closer. Both men were so involved in whatever they were looking at, neither had noticed her enter.

Time to offer her assistance if she could. "Have you found out anything yet?"

"Morgan?"

She jumped back at Carter's surprised bark. "Um...yeah. Who did you think I was?"

His eyes narrowed suspiciously and her stomach gave a nervous upheaval. So far, if she had to choose, she'd lean toward Carter thinking of her as the enemy.

"Where were you?" he demanded.

"Oh." Her cheeks flooded with heat. She couldn't lie to her boss and after all, he did comment on her rather skimpy outfit this morning. He ought to be able to figure out why she'd gone home for God's sake. "Er, I was...changing clothes."

"Changing—" He eyed her up and down, a scowl on his face. "Why?" He sounded thoroughly perplexed.

Perfect. Here she was, standing in front of one of her bosses, the head of their security and a few other uncomfortable-looking co-workers, having to explain why she'd gone home to change. He had to know by now that Ridge had literally dragged her out of here earlier. Hell, he probably knew exactly what they'd been doing while they were gone.

Her cheeks went supernova. Any more and her face would catch fire.

"Do we have to talk about this now?" she muttered.

Carter waved his hand in obvious irritation. "No." Then he beckoned her over and pointed at her screen. "Perhaps you'd care to talk about this then."

She squinted to see more clearly what he was showing her. It was an email program. Her email, in particular. What the heck?

"That's mine," she said unnecessarily.

"I know it is."

She leaned over his shoulder and read the mail on the screen. It didn't look familiar, but then, it was dated today and considering she hadn't been in the office for most of the morning...

"I don't know what I'm looking at, Carter." She had to

admit, she knew her job and how to do it well, but when it came to the ins and outs of computers, she might as well live back in the Stone Age. Sending and answering emails, spreadsheets, reports, calendars and surfing the internet were about the extent of her technological knowledge.

"It's an email to Biggs and Hilliard."

Biggs and Hilliard? She didn't even know anyone over there. Her gaze searched the message and her breathing came to a stop. There were numbers. Big numbers. Ones that looked very much like the bid Malone and Casey had put in for the Honor Center. The nausea swam full force to her throat. Morgan wasn't stupid. She knew now she was public enemy number one.

"I didn't send this, Carter." If he didn't believe her then she had no way of defending herself.

"Any reason someone would want to frame you for this?" He looked skeptical, which made her wonder if he thought she was lying.

"I honestly don't know. Anyone can get to it though, it's right out here in the open."

"You don't have it password protected?"

"I do."

"So anyone *can't* really get to it."

"Well..." Biting her bottom lip, she stepped around him and picked up a Post-It note attached to the side of the monitor. It wasn't visible to the general public, but no one would have to look too hard for it and anyone could have seen her put it there.

Carter hung his head. Apparently he hadn't thought she'd do something so unconscionable or he would have found it by now. "Why?" he asked.

Nothing like your boss making you feel like you were two years old. "Because Ridge said I should change it at least twice a month, and half the time I can't remember what I had to eat for breakfast let alone a new password every two weeks. It's not like I broadcast it over the loudspeaker."

Carter seemed to accept her explanation. "I think Ridge is waiting for you in his office. We'll talk more later."

"I didn't do anything to compromise Malone and Casey, Carter."

Carter stared at her for a moment, then nodded.

She wasn't sure if the motion meant he believed her or he was just trying to appease her for the time being. She hoped it was the former because neither of her bosses was the type she ever wanted to have to go up against.

Morgan wiped her sweaty palms on her thighs before opening Ridge's door. He had to know she was innocent. Didn't he? She'd worked for him for a whole year, and she couldn't remember any time when she'd given him cause to think she'd been anything less than a faithful employee.

Except for today, of course. Would he see what had happened between them as her way of distracting his attention? All the blood left her face. She'd shot from rank of skank to whore. Please God, don't let him think she'd used her body so he wouldn't suspect her.

She opened the door to be greeted by Amy Lee straddling the man whose bed Morgan had shared not two hours ago. The bitch's skirt had ridden up to reveal two round butt cheeks, confirming that Amy Lee did indeed wear a thong. Only a tiny black line could be seen against tan skin.

I haven't had a lover since I hired you.

I'll be ready to take this 'you know' further.

Oh God, had he only been playing with her? She really was going to be sick. For a year she'd tried to work up the courage to make a move for her boss. She'd foolishly thought she'd meant something more to him than another in his line of women. Obviously not. She must have been a damned easy conquest for him. She'd certainly made it easy.

"Morgan."

She jerked at the sound of Ridge's deep voice and found him struggling to get Amy Lee off his lap. She couldn't watch anymore.

The last thing she heard before slamming his door was his garbled, "Get off me."

Angry tears threatened to fall and she choked back the vomit still trying to push its way out. With a sob, she jogged to the front door, ignoring Carter's startled leap from her desk.

"Morgan?" He sounded concerned, but why he should care when he thought she'd sold them out, she didn't know.

She only knew she had to get out of there. Pushing through the door, she ran all the way to her car. Thankfully she'd never put her bag down, so her keys were readily available. If she had left them behind, she would have kept on running until she found the first bus she came to. There was shouting behind her, but she didn't know and didn't care who it came from. As angry and embarrassed as she was, she would probably never find it in her to come back. Let them think she'd been the mole.

Morgan no longer cared.

But she did. And a few minutes into her getaway, she had to wonder if what she'd witnessed in Ridge's office had really been what she was seeing, or what Amy Lee wanted her to.

"Damn it." Ridge punched the doorframe and relished the sharp pain that streaked up his arm from the knuckles. Long after her car tore out of the lot he stood staring down the street. Little fool was going to get herself killed driving like a maniac.

Max's booming voice drew back to the problem at hand. There'd be plenty of time later to go after Morgan and convince her he wanted nothing to do with the woman who'd surprised him by plastering herself on his lap at the most inopportune time.

He hoped there was time anyway. He didn't know what he'd do if Morgan refused to listen.

Ridge narrowed his eyes as he turned and surveyed the chaos that had become his office. Normally he and Carter would be at meetings right now or out at the construction sites of buildings their company had designed. Morgan might be with him or sitting at her desk.

Now Carter occupied her chair, with Amy Lee hovering over his shoulder, and Max sprawled in the chair across the desk from them. He looked relaxed, but Ridge knew the appearance was deceiving. Max was one of those people who could move and in a split second have another man plastered against the wall, his arm bent sharply behind him before he knew what hit him.

Right now his otherwise lazy attention was focused on...

Amy Lee.

Damn. Hadn't she caused enough trouble today? He wouldn't have thought Max would be swayed by a woman dressed to attract every man in a one-hundred-foot radius. He seemed more the discerning type. So why was he watching her so intently? Ridge tried to see what Max did.

Amy Lee was nervous. He wouldn't have noticed if he hadn't been looking for it. She was fidgeting. Her lower lip was tucked between her teeth, and her thumb and forefinger rubbed together. They stopped abruptly as if she'd realized what she was doing, then a small smile tugged at her lips. One manicured hand landed on Carter's shoulder and those fingers went to work with a gentle massage. Carter rolled his head, savoring the favor.

Un-fucking-believable. Five minutes ago she'd been giving Ridge a lap dance, and now she had her claws in Carter.

Max spoke before Ridge could say a word.

"Amy Lee."

She jumped. "Yes?"

One eyebrow lifted lazily. "Do you have something to be nervous about?"

"I don't know what you're talking about." There was a haughty tone to her voice and her chin lifted in regal bearing.

"Then let me ask you this. Do you always try to seduce both your bosses at the same time?"

Amy Lee gasped, Carter turned a narrow-eyed glare at Max and Ridge smiled. He wasn't aware anyone else had known she'd been in his office, but he wasn't surprised Max had worked it out. After all, there was only one way out. She would have had to walk past both men, making it kind of obvious where she'd been. Max, though, had put two and two together.

"I have never—"

"You may want to think long and hard before you answer him, Amy Lee," Ridge said softly.

Her gaze flew to his, as did Carter's, who shrugged off Amy Lee's touch like it was suddenly burning him. "What's going on?"

"I think we've just found our mole." Ridge stuffed his hands in his pockets and leaned against the wall. "Now I want to know why you chose Morgan to frame for your stupidity."

Amy Lee shook her head vigorously.

"What better way to divert attention from yourself than to use your body to entice the men who pay you?" Max remained in his bored slouch, letting things play out around him, but Ridge knew the photographic memory of his was taking notes.

"I—" She broke off and eyed each man in the room.

"Amy Lee?" Carter's voice was deceptively menacing. "If you've got something to say, you better damn well say it. And let me make it clear, I'm pissed about having accused an innocent woman."

Her chin wobbled for a fraction of a second before she composed herself and sniffed. "I didn't have any idea who Richard was when I went to bed with him the first time. It was only later when he said he would pay me to do a little snooping. I needed the money," she implored.

Christ. *For what?* he wanted to shout. "So you sold us out instead of coming to us for help? Do we look like that big of bastards we wouldn't help an employee in trouble? Did we *ever* give you that impression?" He wanted to keep at her but Ridge didn't have time to listen to her sob story. He had more important things to do. Like hunt down his woman and apologize. On his knees if need be.

"I'm sorry," she said, but Ridge didn't see even an ounce of guilt on her face.

He turned his attention to Carter. "I trust you can handle things from here."

Max and Carter nodded.

"Go find Morgan. She looked upset." Carter waved him off. "Who could blame her," he growled, pinning Amy Lee with a glare.

"Upset is an understatement." Ridge centered his anger on Amy Lee. If he lost Morgan over this nonsense, Amy Lee better pray she never crossed paths with him again.

Chapter Six

It took an hour to get his afternoon in order, find Morgan's address, and get there. The hardwood door greeted him like an impenetrable barrier. He only hoped she didn't keep him out too long. There was only so much heartache a man could take. And the worst part was that she hadn't even given him the chance to explain the octopus on his lap, though he could well imagine what she'd thought she was witnessing.

He'd have gone ballistic too if their roles had been reversed. No, strike that. He'd have stormed across the office, yanked the bastard off her lap and put his fist through his eye. But that was neither here nor there because Morgan was a woman and thus prone to getting angry and giving him the silent treatment.

How long did those things last anyway?

No time like the present to find out. Staring at the door would never get him anywhere. He rapped on it and leaned closer, trying to hear her coming. Unless she'd gone for a stress-relieving jog or something, she was home. Her car was parked in the driveway.

Nothing. No sound within. He couldn't even hear a TV or radio. Ridge dropped his forehead to the wood. No doubt she'd peeked out a window, saw him standing there and was now waiting him out.

Then she was in for a long wait. He stepped back and knocked harder, using the meat of his fist.

This time when he put his ear to the door, he heard her.

Still not happy by the sound of her stomping.

"Damn. Oh you sorry son of a b—" She was muffled by the door, but what the hell was going on in there?

His heart racing, Ridge pounded, making the door shake. If he'd had a gun, he would have drawn it and shot the lock off.

"Would you *wait* one dang second?" she yelled.

Ridge cocked his head. That didn't sound like a female in trouble. Pissed off, maybe, but not in trouble.

"Good grief." The door was ripped open to reveal a very surprised, very wet Morgan, wrapped in nothing but a thin robe.

Her skin was flushed. He guessed its pink tone came from a bath or shower. No wonder it had taken a while for her to get to the door.

She gripped the edge of the door with white knuckles. "What?"

Okay, he deserved that. For about five seconds.

"Is there a reason you were cursing just now?"

"Yes."

He waited. Getting no elaboration, he asked, "Care to explain?"

"I stubbed my toe on the end table trying to answer the door someone was pounding on. I thought surely someone had died or was going to if I didn't get here quick. Impatient bastard."

The last words were mumbled but he heard them all the same. He hid a smile. Now probably wasn't a good time to let her think he found her anger humorous.

"Can I come in?"

"Do you smell like her?"

Ridge raised an eyebrow. He kind of liked her angry. Kind of. "If I do, it isn't my fault."

Her shoulders deflated and, dropping her hand to her side,

she blew out a huge breath. "I know."

"You do?"

She stepped back, allowing him entry. "Yes. I figured it out about five minutes after I ran out the door and could make my brain work."

Her skin gave off warmth, and he could smell whatever fruity shampoo she'd used. She had a nice house. He could see through the living room into the kitchen and breakfast area. To the right was a hallway he assumed led to the bedrooms.

"So..."

She sighed. "So I know Amy Lee put herself in your lap. Probably with the knowledge that I would find you there."

A huge weight lifted off his chest. "She's the one who's been selling our bids."

Morgan sank onto the couch and held the lapels of her robe shut with one fist. He itched to pull the damn offending thing off and lick any stray drop of water from her skin that might still be lingering.

"Why?"

Ridge shrugged. "She said she didn't know who Richard Biggs was when she started sleeping with him and that he'd offered money she supposedly needed. I don't know what for, and I split before I heard anymore." He stepped in front of her and sat on the coffee table, encasing her knees between his. "I only had one thing on my mind."

She sniffed and he saw for the first time some puffiness around her eyes. He hated that he'd made her cry.

"I'm sorry, sweetheart."

Morgan nodded and raised her gaze to his. "You thought it was me, didn't you?"

His jaw ticked. "For about twenty seconds. But, see it from my point of view, will you? The woman I'd been pining for for a year, who never made her attraction to me clear, suddenly shows up at work wearing...well, not a lot, and we end up in my bed for some of the most fantastic lovemaking of my life. Then I get a call saying someone in our office is selling bids, and you"—he touched her nose—"say you have this oh-so-important thing you have to do and run off. I get to work and Carter's at your desk. Your computer's filled with evidence that always seemed too pat for my tastes but there was this whole thing with—"

"Me sleeping with you out of the blue and running off, making me look guiltier than hell."

"Pretty much," he admitted. "I didn't believe it for long, but it did cross my mind."

He stared at her, hoping she understood. When she didn't speak, he put his hands on her bare knees and squeezed. He counted it as a good sign that she didn't bat his hands away or cringe.

"Bath or shower?" he whispered. She gasped when his hands slid higher, delving beneath the robe's hem.

"Bath. I was stinky."

"Yeah? How come?"

"Went for a run."

"Stress relief?" His fingertips brushed her pubic hair.

"Yep." Her head fell back on the couch, exposing the long column of her throat.

"Because of me?"

"No."

"No?"

"Because of her." Her head snapped up. "Can we not talk about her right now?" In a bold move, she grabbed his hand, spread her legs as wide as his would let her and covered her naked mound with his palm.

"Yes, ma'am." He wasn't stupid. With his free hand, Ridge untied the belt at her waist and separated the fabric. Smooth, creamy skin appeared, and it was all his. He leaned in and kissed his way from the top of her pubic bone to her chin,

60

licking along her throat when she displayed it again.

Not one to neglect a woman's body, he caressed her breast as he melded their lips together. She squirmed beneath him, opening herself up to him.

"Make love to me," she rasped, attacking the buttons of his shirt until they popped off and flew across the room to click on the hardwood floor.

He had to remove his hand from her pussy to tug his shirt off his shoulders and pull it out of his pants. He threw it over his back. Her fingers wrestled with his belt and zipper, but she took too long.

Pushing her hands aside, he growled, "Let me." In record time he shucked his shoes, pants, underwear and socks, tossing them to join his shirt.

Her hand wrapped around his erection, making him hiss. Her lips followed before he could stop her and she sucked him deep.

"Ah, fuck." He held her head in his hands, trying to keep her still while she did her best to suck the come from his balls. His legs shook, his breath heaved in and out. "You gotta stop, Morgan."

Her gaze met his and damn if it wasn't the most erotic thing he'd ever seen. Her cheeks hollowed around his cock.

"Christ." With supreme effort, he forced her off then followed her down on the couch, stretching them out and fitting between her thighs like he belonged there.

"Yes." Her back arched when the tip of his cock touched her entrance, slick with her juices. Hot, *wet* juices.

"Shit." He dropped his forehead on hers.

"What?"

"No condom." He leapt away and scrambled after his pants. There had to be one more. "Yes." He ripped the foil with his teeth and rolled the rubber on before rejoining her.

She giggled at him.

"This is no laughing matter."

"You're very enthusiastic."

"For you? Hell yeah. I told you I've waited a long time. Better get used to it."

Her eyes widened. "Used to it?"

"Absolutely. I figure it'll take me about...sixty years to get you out of my system."

"Ridge?"

"Yes, sweetheart."

"Tell me I'm not dreaming."

He took one of her nipples between his thumb and forefinger and pinched it. Her initial squeak turned into a moan when he bent and drew the hardened peak into his mouth.

He released her after a strong last tug. "Nope, you're not dreaming."

"If I am, this is the best dream I've ever had."

He guided his erection to the sweet opening between her legs once more. Now he wished he hadn't had a condom. He wanted more than anything to take her *au naturel* and make her completely his by spilling his come inside her.

"I know it's the best one I've ever had," he murmured, and entered her in one thrust. He forced himself to stay perfectly still, relishing the sensation of her tiny muscles squeezing him. Her ankles locked together at the small of his back and her hands went to his shoulders. Already he felt her claws unsheathed.

Suited him just fine. *Any* way she responded to him suited him just fine. So long as she always did. He didn't know when it had happened, but at some point in the last year he'd fallen in love with her.

"Move." She pulled him tight against her with those fantastic legs he wouldn't let her hide anymore.

"I'm trying not to explode before we've even started," he

panted.

"But I need you to move."

"Pushy."

"You haven't seen pushy yet."

Ridge started a slow rhythm, withdrawing almost all the way before sliding back in as deep as he could go. He couldn't get close enough. Sweat beaded his forehead and his heart hammered. She countered his thrust with her own and sobbed when she didn't get what she wanted.

"Please, can we dispense with the slow and easy?" she cried, tilting her head back.

Ridge licked along her pulse, up her jaw and nibbled at her earlobe. "Slow and steady wins the race."

She jerked her chin down and glared at him. "Slow and steady isn't getting me an orgasm."

He grinned, but reached a hand between their bodies to slide his thumb over the bundle of nerves peeking out of its folds.

"Yeeessss."

"You're easy."

She licked her lips. "Only with you."

"Damn straight."

Her hips shifted, seeking more contact, and he gave it to her. He'd had enough himself. With a frenzy of hammering hips, he took her. Every little noise, grunt and moan spurred him on. His balls were taut and a tingle worked its way from the base of his spine.

"Come with me," he urged. Her teeth found the skin between his neck and shoulder and she bit down. It was all the incentive he needed, not that he needed much. The tingle that began down deep spread the length of his erection and exploded out the top. Every muscle in his body grew rigid as he emptied himself inside his woman.

His woman. Without a doubt. If she thought for one second he was going to let her go, she was crazy.

Bracing himself on his elbows, Ridge lowered his body to hers. The hard peaks of her nipples stabbed into his chest, and the only noise to be heard was the harsh rush of breath from their lungs.

"Please tell me we don't have to use a condom ever again," he whispered in her ear, biting gently on the lobe.

"Ever? 'Cause, I'd kinda like to have some sort of break between babies."

Ridge lifted his head and stared at her in wonder. "You said it and now you can't take it back."

Her lip disappeared between her teeth. "I don't want to take it back."

"So you'll marry me?" His heart thudded, and not because of the energy they'd just expended.

"That depends."

"On?" She was killing him here.

"Do I have to take orders from you *all* the time?"

He shifted his hips, reveling in the wet heat still surrounding his cock and grinning at the gasp that pushed past her lips.

"Only at work."

Her face turned thoughtful for a bit too long. Ridge reached down and pinched her ass.

"Ouch," she squeaked. When she still didn't answer, he raked his fingers along her side, making her squirm and laugh. Every time she moved, his cock hardened further inside her. "Okay, okay. Uncle."

"Don't ever mistake me for your uncle, sweetheart."

"Never." She smiled, wrapped her arms around his neck and pulled him down for a kiss. "Yes."

"Talk about keeping a man in suspense," he grumbled,

rubbing his nose on hers. "I love you, Morgan."

"I didn't really expect this to happen when I was getting dressed this morning."

"I'm glad it did."

"Me too. Can we do it again?"

He groaned and dropped his forehead to hers. "I've created a monster." He was obviously going to have to work on his stamina to keep up with the insatiable creature below him.

She giggled, and with an amazing show of speed and strength had their positions reversed. Hands braced on his chest, she bent to kiss him again before growling, "Rarrrr."

Bridging the Gap

Dedication

To my critique group, CORE, thank you for your help and support, especially to Shane who let all us women know that sitting on a leather couch post sex wouldn't be the best thing in the world to do...

To my slave driver, Leila Brown, who basically whips me every time I leave my seat—she's worse than a drill sergeant but man, she gets me through it with her timed drills that I can't stand to lose.

To the Life Flight nurse for his information, which totally blew me away—thank you sooo much.

And to my editor, Sasha, for never giving up on me. Thank you!

Chapter One

"Shit. Shit. Don't stop. Gaaawd." Ryan Cooper bit her lip and dug her heels into the mattress while the man between her legs continued wreaking havoc on her clit. Carter alternated between stabbing his tongue into her opening and flicking at the taut bundle of nerves. Three times already he'd brought her to the peak only to back off before she crossed over.

No freakin' way was he going to get away with it this time.

In the dim light, she reached for his head, tangled her fingers in his mussed blond hair and held him to her.

"You stop this time and I swear you'll have to pull your balls out of your throat."

He chuckled, but before she could cuff him upside the head, he blew a raspberry against her clit that had her squeezing her eyes shut, her back arching and stars flaring behind her eyelids.

She couldn't speak. Hell, she couldn't breathe. Couldn't do anything but hold her rigid posture as her clit pounded with every quickened heartbeat.

A few minutes ago she hadn't been able to get the man to finish her. Now she was paralyzed to do anything against his continued assault on her throbbing pussy except try to decapitate him with her thighs.

Moments later when the aftershocks had finally subsided, Carter still lapped at her as if he were a kitten leisurely sipping its milk. Her thighs parted, her knees collapsed to the mattress and slowly but surely, Ryan extracted her fingers from his hair.

If he thought for one second she'd be able to reciprocate anytime soon...

The bed dipped between her legs and Carter's forearms slipped beneath her knees, lifting them in the crooks of his elbows. She sucked in a breath as the head of his already-covered penis pressed into her, setting off another wave of tingles through her clit.

She bit her lip as the pressure built inside. Her vaginal muscles stretched to accommodate his thickness. Lubrication wasn't an issue, not after the climax she'd just had, but Carter was no small man. He had big hands, big feet and his cock, well, his cock went the way of the cliché.

"Easy, babe." Carter held her hips as he worked himself deeper, spreading her to what seemed an impossible width.

She loved the feel of him inside, loved that he seemed to know when to back off and when to push further. His thumbs traced her hipbones, soothing the flare of heat that accompanied his penetration. The hair on his thighs tickled the backs of hers. His hips moved forward, her pussy sucked another inch in. There couldn't possibly be any more room.

Carter proved her thoughts wrong. He leaned over, bringing her legs up and nearly folding her in half. The act imbedded his penis inside her. His pelvis pressed against her clit.

The moment of bliss. Eyes crossed, Ryan threw her head back. His lips caressed her throat, teased over her collarbone, trailed down between her barely there breasts then centered on one, latching onto the nipple to suckle while he held himself immobile deep in her channel. He drew on the nipple, sucking strongly before releasing it with a pop, and she wondered for an insane second if it were possible to extract milk from a non-lactating woman.

Then all thoughts ceased.

Carter withdrew and Ryan scrambled to keep him from

pulling out completely. She reached between her legs to grasp his waist and hold him close.

"Uh-uh," he grunted above her, his eyes glittering with desire. Releasing one leg, he gathered her arms and positioned them over her head, where he held her wrists together. "Leave them, or I stop."

"You do not play fair."

"All's fair in love and war, babe."

"So is this love or war?"

"You don't leave those hands there, it'll be war." A drop of sweat landed on her cheek, just below her eye.

"Gross."

"Sex is sweaty business, sweetheart, just like love and war." He grinned and shifted his hips, pressing in once more, right where she wanted him.

Why in the hell was she arguing with the first man who'd ever made her orgasm without the use of her own hand?

"Staying." The word spat from her lips when the head of his cock hit a particularly sweet spot. She bared her throat to him yet again. "Don't stop."

"Don't move your hands."

"Won't."

Reduced to one-word phrases. He did this to her every time she graced his bed. Or his floor. Or his table.

Had they really only known each other for two weeks? Felt like years the way they'd connected so instantly. Until him she had never jumped into bed with a man she'd only just met, never slept with a man after the very first date.

He rotated his hips, making her body scream in need-to-have-more.

"Please?" And there's the begging.

"Please what?" Damn him for being so calm.

"More." And the head-spinning-around Exorcist-style growl.

Why in the hell did he bother with her?

When he smiled, his teeth flashed in the soft glow from the cracked-open bathroom door.

"My turn." At least he'd been reduced to the same gravelly tone she had. Now the fun would begin.

Carter pistoned in and out, somehow managing to hit her clit with every penctration. Ryan fisted her hands and forced herself not to move them. The ass was sadistic enough to stop the second she did. She'd found that out the first night. He'd left her hanging until she'd been reduced to begging and then he'd had the nerve to tie her wrists to the headboard, ensuring she couldn't move.

She bit her lip. Damn thing would be bloody soon. Her vagina stretched around him, tears sprang from the corners of her eyes and her small breasts miraculously bounced with every thrust.

Who'd have ever thought she'd go for that submissive shit?

She could tell he was close. His eyes slid shut, his lips pursed and his nostrils flared. Every single time. He had ten seconds at most.

Ryan knew just how to retaliate. She flexed her Kegels, effectively squeezing Carter's cock, and was rewarded with his hiss and a pause in thrusts. He promptly sought revenge by placing his thumb on her clit and rubbing in a tight circle. The bundle of nerves, already so close to rocketing off once more, spasmed.

"Shiiiiit." Ryan twisted the bedspread in her fingers and arched beneath Carter, burying his cock even further, and all thoughts of forcing his ejaculation flew out the window. Left paralyzed a second time, there was nothing for her to do but succumb to his thrusts and the slick abrasion of his pelvis on her clit.

A moment later he too became rigid, gripping her hips to him as if he were afraid of falling out, and the pulse of his climax beat with her own.

He collapsed on her, both of them breathing heavy.

Aware that he was smashing the beautiful woman beneath him, Carter Malone slowly extracted himself from the tight sheath still gripping his cock and rolled to his side. Ryan groaned with what he hoped was reluctance to let him go. He removed the spent condom, reached for a tissue to wrap it in and dropped it on the floor to deal with later, then fell to his back.

She was consuming him alive. Two weeks into their...dating—is that what she would call their relationship? Because there hadn't been many *dates*—and he was already more aware of her than he'd ever been about any other woman. And if he knew a lot about anything other than architecture, it was women. Precious, soft, *willing* women. He didn't get off on forcing them to do his bidding, though tying one up now and then might add to the sexual tension.

He wondered what Ryan would think of the direction his thoughts had gone. Would she run? Profess her undying love? Invite him to seek the advice of a psychologist?

Hell, what was he thinking? Outside of fucking, he didn't know a great deal about her. They'd literally bumped into each other at a charity event he'd attended at his mother's request. He didn't even remember what the hell the event had been held for. Raising money for some affliction or another. From there they'd ended up at her place, something he was sure she'd either A) never done before or B) if she had, rarely. He had the feeling he was her first. Not partner, but taking a man home immediately after meeting him.

Made him feel possessive as all shit.

Carter rubbed a hand over his face as his breathing finally subsided into a more normal rhythm. He must be getting old.

Jesus. Was his clock ticking? Did that happen to men?

"I think I'm dead," she groaned next to him.

He smiled and propped himself on his elbow. Unable to resist, he ran his fingertips over the sweat-slicked skin between her breasts. Her nipples puckered and she shivered. "Nah. If you were dead, we wouldn't be able to do that again, and that would be a damn shame."

She lifted her head and glanced down his torso to find his dick echoing his words and hardening.

"Right this second?"

Carter laughed at the incredulous look on her face. "I'll give you a few minutes recovery time first."

"You're so gracious." She sighed and threw an arm over her eyes. "I have to get up."

"Bathroom?"

"That too."

Thank God the fact her face was covered hid his confusion. What other reason would she have to get up? "You got a hot date?"

"Yep. With my bed." She dragged herself to a sitting position and Carter swallowed.

Why should he care if she wanted to run out on him? He typically led his dates back to their house so he could make the getaway before things got to the point of wanting to stay the night.

"I was kinda thinking you might stay the night." *Pathetic, man. Pathetic.*

"I can't. Have to start a new job tomorrow which requires sleep. Staying the night here might net me an hour, two tops, knowing you." A sly smile split her lips and succeeded in completely renewing his erection.

Carter leaned forward and licked a pert nipple. It shouldn't be too hard to convince her to stay. They definitely had chemistry between them even if they didn't know too many other aspects of each other's lives.

She pushed his head away, giggling. "Don't think you can

74

distract me, Carter."

"Damn it." He trailed his fingers down her abdomen and across her hip when she rose. Sweaty blonde bangs clung to her forehead. The rest of her shoulder-length hair she gathered in one hand while she fanned her neck with the other. He loved that she didn't try and hide her body from him. The idea was pointless really since he'd more than looked at every millimeter of her skin.

He'd nibbled, tasted, kissed, licked, bit, touched and smelled all of it. She was his addiction and he wanted more.

His fingers itched to pull her tall, slender body back to the bed. He'd kind of shocked himself being attracted to her. He usually gravitated toward women with a little more build, more voluptuous breasts for sure. Ryan's breasts weren't even what he'd call a handful, but damn if they didn't respond to the slightest touch.

She cleared her throat, drawing his attention to her face where her pale blue eyes glittered in mischief.

"You're staring."

"Yep. And they"—he nodded toward her breasts—"would like to play some more."

"They might *want* to but they aren't going to get to."

"Damn it."

She looked back over her shoulder as she headed for the restroom. "You've said that already."

"I mean it. And it's not nice to keep a man hanging like this," he called then collapsed onto his back. Where had he gone wrong? He didn't normally cause women to feel the need to run off the minute he pulled out.

"I hardly see anything *hanging*. Perhaps standing is a better word," she said through the crack of the door.

The toilet flushed and water ran before she returned, naked and swaying her hips.

"If you're wanting to leave, then perhaps you should stop

trying to tempt me."

"Me walking is tempting?" She dropped to her hands and knees. "Where the hell is my underwear?"

"Everything you do is tempting, babe." Jesus Christ, didn't she realize what that particular position made him think of?

"Oh yeah?" She shook her ass.

"Son of a bitch." Carter launched himself off the bed and knelt behind that wiggling backside to press his cock against her folds. Little nymph knew exactly what she was doing.

Ryan squealed and jerked in his hands, but he held fast to her hips.

"You better be damn glad there isn't a condom in my hand or you wouldn't be leaving right now."

She lowered her head to the floor, and in the light spilling from the bathroom, he saw her suck her lower lip in. She looked like the perfect little submissive. He ran his index finger down the length of her spine, between the crease of her buttocks, over the rosy aperture and then to her opening. Gathering the wetness there, he slipped further and circled her clit. Ryan moaned and arched her back into his touch.

He had her.

"No." Ryan jerked upright and twisted, shaking a finger at him. "No, no and no. That was just mean."

"Damn it."

She snorted at him. *Snorted.* "You're in a rut."

"No, I want to be in rut."

She smacked his chest and leaped to her feet when he grabbed for her. "Insatiable."

"Yes." He nodded vigorously and crawled toward her.

Son of a bitch. He was on the floor fucking crawling after a woman. Carter slowly gained his feet and palmed his straining and very disappointed dick. The look in Ryan's eyes said she was trying not to laugh.

"Tell me again what's so all-fire important you can't stay the night?"

"Work. New job, mister."

"I'll set the alarm."

"No."

"I'll make you breakfast." Crawling and begging. Is this what pussy-whipped felt like?

"In bed?" She cocked an eyebrow and a hip. He had her.

"Absolutely."

"No."

"Damn it."

This time she did laugh and the sound went straight to his cock. Which he was still friggin' holding. He crossed his arms over his chest. Ryan had found all her clothing and was calmly dressing as if nothing was wrong.

"There's someone else isn't there?"

She glanced up at him from putting her sock on. "Yes."

Jealousy smacked him between the eyes. "I knew it."

Ryan straightened and once more he could tell she was trying not to laugh. "My father."

Well, shit. And then he got concerned. "You're not...um, I mean, you know..."

"Eww." He received another smack, this one on his bare shoulder, which stung like hell. "I work for him, stupid."

"I knew that."

"Uh-huh." Her disbelieving tone said it all. "Just when would I have had time to find another lover in the last two weeks? Between your job and mine we've spent every free night together. And I haven't stayed the night yet so what makes this night any different?"

Carter wrapped his arms around her waist, despising the clothes she'd donned, and nuzzled the skin below her left ear. "Because I want you to."

She leaned back so she could look him in the eye. "Aw. I want to too." She shoved him away. "Just not tonight. New job, need sleep, not gonna get it here."

"What is this new job?"

Ryan bent to slip her tennis shoes on. "I'm just helping my dad out for a while. Filling in 'til he gets someone else."

"How 'bout Friday night?" *More begging, Malone?*

Shoes tied, she came over to him and patted his chest. "Friday sounds good. Here or my place?"

"Here," he growled, yanking her closer and kissing her deep. "That way I can keep you locked up and not let you out of my bed 'til I'm good and ready."

"I can't wait." The way her pupils dilated proved she couldn't.

Good. He wouldn't be the only one miserable all week. She kissed him this time, slipping her tongue into his mouth and feasting on him like she couldn't get enough.

"Seriously," he said, panting hard. "If you want to leave, you need to stop. Otherwise those clothes are coming off and I'll have you flat on your back."

She sighed. "I'm going, I'm going."

He followed her, naked, to the front door, uncaring about the state of his undress. His home was isolated enough, set back off the road and surrounded on two sides by woods and the third by a lake, that he wasn't worried about being seen even if he paraded around outside in the buff.

With one last peck on his lips, Ryan jogged down the three steps of his porch and headed for her car.

"Be careful driving home, babe."

"I will." She waved to him and got into her sensible little Toyota Corolla.

The car was newer but still, he wished she drove something a tad more safe. Like an Expedition, or a Land Cruiser. A tank would be nice. Maybe he could get her one...

"Jesus, Malone. Two weeks. You've been seeing the woman two weeks," he muttered, slamming the door shut when her taillights disappeared over the rise. "A bit early to be thinking about buying her a car, or marriage, or getting her pregnant, don't you think?"

Carter walked over and gripped the back of the leather sofa gracing his open living room, then dropped his head forward.

He was in so much trouble.

Chapter Two

Carter stepped into his office Monday morning after having slept a total of two hours. Half his brain kept trying to determine why Ryan had practically run out on him, job or no job, while the other half had wondered why he should care. No amount of coffee had perked him up this morning, but the sight of his partner Ridge Casey's wife, Morgan, pregnant and glowing with it, sure the hell did.

He needed a psychiatrist if he was jealous of what his partner had that he didn't.

The closer he got, Carter realized Morgan's cheeks were puffed and rosy, her hair mussed and her clothes in disarray. If it weren't for the prominent bulge of her belly signifying late pregnancy, Carter would say she'd just been thoroughly fucked by her husband in Ridge's office.

"Morg, if you don't go into labor soon, I'm afraid you might pop." He spoke the same words he used every morning upon seeing her.

This particular morning, to his utter dismay, her eyes welled with tears instead of her normal grin and, "Shut the hell up."

Horse's ass. "Shit. I'm sorry, Morg." He strode closer and attempted to give her a gentle hug.

"Don't touch me," she snapped, anger replacing the tears.

Carter reared back. Had he entered an alternate universe?

What in the shit had happened to the normally quiet, sweet woman who graced their front office? Maybe he was still asleep. Dreaming? Nightmare, more like it.

"Oh good, you're here." Ridge rushed from his office, papers a jumbled mess in his hands, some of them falling to the floor behind him.

Definitely not awake. His partner never acted this way unless there was an emer...gency— He swung back to Morgan. "Are you in labor?"

"Yes." Ridge barked his answer at the same time Morgan gave a terrified nod, one hand going to her belly.

"What the hell are you doing here then?" Carter snatched the pile of papers from Ridge's hands and slapped them down on Morgan's desk.

"We're leaving. Her water broke about ten minutes ago, and I'm running around here trying to get this shit in order for you."

"For God's sake, Ridge, they invented cell phones a few years back. Use it and get the hell out of here."

"I am, I, we—"

"What he means," Morgan said, calmly reaching for her purse and the carryall they'd packed and brought to the office just in case something happened at work, "is that we were just getting ready to head out the door." Her sedate attitude had both men looking at her.

Tears, pissed off, serene in the space of two minutes. Were all women in labor like this? Would Ryan be?

Shit! Stop thinking about her.

He blinked as Morgan took a deep breath, closed her eyes and smiled at some inner secret apparently only she was privy to. The strangeness had him thinking of the music from the *X-Files—doo, doo, doo, doo, doo, doo...*

"Right. What she said." Ridge patted every pocket on his body, twice. Morgan cleared her throat and held out the keys between her forefinger and thumb. Ridge grabbed them. "I knew you had them."

Morgan hummed in response. Carter had never seen his best friend so flustered. He kind of enjoyed it. He'd enjoy razzing him later even more.

Settling himself against Morgan's desk, he crossed his arms over his chest and sat back to watch the man disintegrate.

Ridge ushered his lovely wife across the room, mumbling something that sounded like, "Do we have everything?" He stopped and snapped his fingers as Morgan pushed on the door.

"Damn. I almost forgot. You need to go over to the Wellingby site and meet with the new foreman."

Carter nodded. "Can do."

"I'm supposed to go, but...Ryan Dixon is his name, I think. He's Mr. Dixon's son."

Carter's heart rate shot through the roof at the name Ryan. Ryan Dixon, not Ryan Cooper. Man, not woman. Still, the name made him imagine her creamy skin beneath his fingertips, the way her nipples peaked under his tongue, the way her pussy hugged his cock so tight it made his eyes cross.

"Carter."

"What?" He shook the vision of Ryan's body undulating with his from his mind and forced himself not to adjust his cock beneath the zipper of his khakis.

"Jesus, man, you're more lost than I am."

"Yeah. I don't think that's possible."

Morgan waved. "Hello? Pregnant woman nearly about to birth your child in the office waiting here."

"Shit." Ridge turned again to his wife then once more back to Carter. "Ryan. Foreman. Go. Meet."

"Yes, yes. I will. I'll go now in fact." He pulled his keys from his pocket and followed them out. "Call me the second you know anything. And good luck, Morg. Don't let Ridge flip out on you."

"Too late," she announced over the doorframe before it shut.

Carter laughed and hopped in his SUV, ready to fulfill Ridge's wishes lest he cause the man a coronary on the day of his first child's birth. He tried to remember what he knew about the Wellingby site. The project was one of Ridge's babies, his conception, and while Carter had collaborated on it, he had his own projects going at the same time. He knew the former foreman had broken his leg in an on-site accident, and Ridge had said the owner of the construction company had someone to replace him temporarily until the man was able to come back. And from what Carter could recall, it would be awhile until the other man was able to return to work since his injuries were pretty extensive.

A measure of adrenaline raced through his system. Carter loved going to the job sites, loved seeing their projects come to fruition from the ground up. The Wellingby site would be gorgeous. State-of-the-art facility for patrons of the arts from toddlers to the elderly. It was going to be a welcome addition to the community, graciously donated by the Wellingby family.

Twenty minutes later, Carter pulled onto the gravel entrance. The site was in full swing even this early in the morning, like a beehive of activity with yellow hard-hat-wearing workers crawling all over the infrastructure of steel beams. He turned into a section reserved for the workers' vehicles and sat, watching, window down, still unable to believe what he did for a living had a part in creating the vast building being constructed right before his eyes.

The hum and whir of machinery combined with the near-constant knocking of hammers, and the buzz of saws almost overrode the shouts and calls of the workers. He missed it. Architecture was his passion but construction was how he'd made his way through college. His father had been a laborer. Carter had practically cut his teeth chewing on his daddy's tools. He loved sitting four stories up and feeling the steel between his legs, no pun intended, as he attached two beams together.

He sighed. Wouldn't happen today. Two trailers were parked to the right of his position. Inside he'd likely find the new foreman, but his fingers itched to get more hands on and join in the fun of building instead of overseeing and planning.

"Hell." He jerked the keys from the ignition and got out. All this wishing. He was beginning to feel like a girl.

As he walked to the back of the SUV to retrieve his hard hat, gravel crunched beneath the steel-toed Redwing boots he always wore in case he was needed at a site. At least he'd get to look a little bit the part with his boots and hat. The khakis, dress shirt and tie threw the rest out of whack. Anyone with half a brain would know he hadn't come there to pound nails.

The door to the trailer opened just as he reached for it and a man stepped out, nodding to him in acknowledgement. Carter stepped back to let him pass and his knees nearly buckled when a sweet, familiar voice rang out.

"And don't forget the dimension change on the south face of—"

"I gotcha, boss," the man said, adjusting his hat on his head.

Carter's cock twitched. He could not have heard her voice. She was at work. A new job. Working for her father. He closed his eyes and swallowed back the rush of unease before stepping up into the brightly lit space to be greeted by the rounded backside of the woman he'd made love to not even twelve hours ago. She spoke on the phone tucked between her shoulder and ear, oblivious to his presence, a white hard hat on her head. A secretary perhaps? He ground his teeth in frustration.

Ryan Dixon, his ass. She'd told him her name was Ryan Cooper. Had Ridge fucked up or had she, for whatever reason, led him astray? Had she known who he was and somehow thought sleeping with him would help her get ahead? And if she'd lied about her name, how many times had she lied to him about other things?

Jesus. Nothing made sense. Sleeping with him wouldn't get her a job. He wasn't even her boss. If anything, she'd answer to the construction owner—apparently her father—and beyond that she'd have to deal with Ridge.

She shifted, wagging that perfect ass in front of him, enticing him to bend her over the OCD clean desk that had a place for everything and everything in its place, and pump his cock in and out of what he knew would be a slick, tight sheath. The other temptation was to throw her facedown over his knee and paddle said perfect ass with his bare hand.

"Yes, Tom." She paused and stuffed a slender hand in her back pocket. "No, I haven't seen him yet. I'll be sure and tell him when I do."

Carter waited not quite so patiently for her to finish her conversation with whoever she spoke to and stayed well on the other side of the trailer from her. If he got too close, no telling what might happen.

"See you then. Bye."

See you then? Like hell she'd see him *then.* The only man she'd be seeing was Carter. The tips of his ears grew hot as jealousy swam through him. Great. First the car and marriage, and now the great green-eyed monster had taken hold of his body.

He wasn't through with her yet. Deceit or not. He cleared his throat.

"Are you back already, Jason?" She turned, then shrieked, throwing a coffee mug she'd been holding in the air. It dropped to the ground with a thunk, the liquid sloshing out to drown everything in sight, including her shirt. "Carter?" The name gurgled from her mouth as the hot coffee soaked through the cotton fabric of two shirts to singe her abdomen.

"Shit." He crossed the space in about four steps to reach for her.

85

Ryan plucked at the button-down shirt and T-shirt underneath. "What are you doing here?" And why was she squeaking?

"I think the more important question is what are *you* doing here?" The accusation in his voice threw her.

"Working for my father, remember? It's why I couldn't stay the night, you ass. Don't go all caveman on me."

"What?" He stepped closer and the warm, male scent of his skin overrode the mocha-sweet smell of the brew she couldn't function without. She didn't give a rat's ass about those who wanted to poison themselves with the caffeinated crap, but the decaf...that was all hers.

Jesus, she was standing here thinking about coffee while a none-too-happy Carter growled down at her.

And oh goodness did he look hot in a hard hat and tie.

"Carter," she said again, trying to come up with some plausible explanation as to why the man she'd been making love to had known where to find her.

"That's my name, *Ryan*."

Eyes wide, she stared at him. He was pissed. At her. "Did you get up on the wrong side of the bed or something, or was it just that I didn't stay the night?"

"It has nothing to do with you not staying the night. It's more about you lying to me for the last two weeks."

She gasped. "Lying? What lie? What are you talking about?"

"What about your name? Ryan Cooper?"

"Uh, yeah, that's my name. Don't wear it out." He had to be stoned. There was no other explanation for the sudden turn in his attitude.

"Then why the fuck did my partner send me here to meet a Ryan Dixon?"

"Dix—oh." Her eyes crinkled in confusion. "Partner?"

"Don't change the subject."

Had she? She was tempted to put a hand on his forehead to see if he had a fever, but touching him would no doubt lead to doing bad things on her desk. So she did the next best thing.

"Are you feeling all right?"

"Answer the question." His nose almost bumped hers as he leaned in menacingly. The only thing preventing it was their hard hats. He couldn't get that close to her. The plastic rim of his hat clipped hers. Bastard didn't even say sorry, but at least he backed off half an inch, leaving her wondering if her eyes were still crossed from having to look at his face while he was practically inside her.

She could hardly breathe from wanting his lips on hers. All this accusing and not even a, "Hi, honey, I'm home."

"What were we talking about?" Ryan swallowed and stared at his mouth, unashamed at how husky her voice sounded.

"Dixon."

"Oh, right. Tom Dixon is my father."

"You told me your name was Cooper."

She nodded. "It is. Tom is my stepfather. I'm not sure why your...partner said my name was Dixon. Who is he by the way? Partner in what, and why, exactly, are you here again?"

A light seemed to go off in his head and a muscle ticked on the side of his face. Made that square jaw so cute. She wanted to nibble on it.

The band in her hard hat must be way too tight.

"Damn it."

She hid her smile at his favorite curse. "What?"

Carter sucked in a breath and rubbed at the back of his neck, a gesture she'd seen him do often. "My partner is Ridge Casey. His wife went into labor this morning so perhaps, in his flustered state of mind, he got the name wrong."

"Wait a minute." Ridge Casey. Carter Malone. Malone and...

She frowned at him. "No. No, no and no. Please don't tell

me you're *that* Carter Malone? From Malone and Casey? The firm that designed this building?" *Please don't tell me I'm that unlucky.*

"Got it in one." He sounded a tad disgusted which only served to confuse her more. Somebody had to have spit in his eggs this morning. Although if she'd been a waitress and he'd come into her restaurant all pissy like he was right now, she'd have done the same.

In hindsight, sleeping with one of the architects did look *really* bad. "Ah hell." Why in the fig hadn't she connected his name? There couldn't possibly be that many Carter Malones in the area. Stupid didn't even begin to encompass the depth of her dumbness.

To keep busy, and hopefully to look less flustered than she felt, Ryan went about setting her hat on the desk and unbuttoning her shirt.

"What are you doing?" He yanked her hands off the buttons.

She pursed her lips. "Changing my shirt. In case you hadn't noticed, you made me ruin this one. I can't very well run around outside soaked in coffee, now can I?" Although she wouldn't mind taking it off and doing other things inside. But since Carter looked like he'd rather do anything than be cooped up with her in the trailer, she went for simply changing.

"Sorry," he mumbled, thumbing the pulse at her wrist for a moment before letting her go.

"It's fine. I've got extras here. Lots to get into out there, ya know?" She stripped off the button-down and blew out a breath at the long-sleeve shirt underneath. It would have to go too. There were extras in the bottom drawer of the desk, ones she'd only placed there this morning. She was suddenly glad she'd come prepared.

After taking the clothing from her stash, she stood to remove the T-shirt. Carter was on her again. This time he grabbed her wrist and held it up for inspection. Ryan licked her lips and prayed he wouldn't ask her about the bracelet.

"What the hell is this?"

God must have been busy. She tried to wiggle out of his grasp, but he held fast.

"Ryan?" His gaze flicked to hers, a million questions flitting through his eyes and making her squirm.

His eyes slid shut as though he was searching for patience. Then he opened them and calmly flipped the small, football-shaped, stainless-steel medallion over and discovered all of her secrets.

"Epilepsy." His lips moved but there wasn't much sound to be heard.

She jerked her hand out of his. Silence reigned while she finished switching shirts. Only when she had herself situated did she finally look at him again. His jaw ticked away with what most likely amounted to anger, but there was sadness on his face. She hated that pity. Had since she was a kid.

"Did you think that was something I didn't need to know about?" he asked quietly.

"No." Dang it, she did not need to defend herself. "It's just not something I broadcast. The bracelet was with me all along. *If* something had happened, and that's a big if since I'm on medication and haven't had an episode in almost two years, then the bracelet and my entire life's information is right in my wallet."

You weren't going to defend yourself, dummy.

His eyes flashed and his nostrils flared. "But that's not something I would have known, is it?"

She rounded on him. "In case of an emergency you wouldn't have handed over my wallet to the police or paramedics?"

"You should have told me."

"Do you know what happened the last time I told a man I was an epileptic on our first date? He gave me the hairy eyeball, his entire body shivered like I'd told him I had a penis as well as a vagina, he gulped down the beer he'd just ordered, and he ran as fast as his cowardly legs could carry him, so no, I don't tell everyone what I have. Excuse the hell out of me."

Carter shoved his fingers through his hair, making the short strands stand on end. "Is this a job you should be working with this condition?"

"Oh. Oh, don't even go there, buster. Do not think for one minute you can tell me what not to do because you've fucked me."

He pushed into her space, nose to nose once more, this time succeeding because he yanked his hat off and she didn't have hers as protection anymore. "Maybe I just don't want to get called one day saying the woman I've been *making love* to had a seizure four stories up and is now hanging by her lifeline."

Well hell. Since he put it that way...

Chapter Three

The door opening behind him kept Carter from saying what he really wanted to, that he couldn't even come close to imagining how he would feel should he get a call one day telling him she'd fallen or gotten hurt.

"Hey, cuz." A tall, lanky man entered the trailer, a goofy grin on his face.

Ryan swiped at her shirt and cleared her throat. She narrowed her eyes at Carter before turning her attention to the new arrival. "Tad." She acknowledged him with a semi-smile, nothing like the one *Tad* graced her with.

Carter ground his teeth together to keep from punching the man in the nose when he kissed Ryan's cheek. Cousin or not, Carter didn't like the sight of another man so close to his woman.

Shit. There you go again, Car.

"Your dad coming in today?" Tad asked, swiping the hard hat from his head and using the long sleeve of his shirt to wipe the sweat from his brow. He moved to the coffee and poured himself a cup.

"Yes." Ryan busied herself folding the coffee-drenched shirt. "He's looking for you actually. I told him I'd tell you to stay put so he could talk to you when he gets here. So, stay put."

Tad flashed another grin over his shoulder as he doctored

his coffee. "Yes, ma'am."

"You better not be drinking my decaf, boy."

"Trust me. I value my balls enough not to touch your shit, dear cousin."

Irritation threatened to strangle Carter. If he threw her cousin out the door, would he piss her off?

"Who's he?" Tad thumbed over his shoulder in Carter's direction.

"He's the man who designed the building you're working on." Ryan peeked at Carter from beneath her long lashes. The same way she looked at him after she'd come in his mouth.

His dick hardened despite the gravity of the situation. Fucking *epilepsy*. And she was working at a construction site. Granted, he didn't know shit about epilepsy except that it caused seizures, but he did know seizures and heavy equipment didn't go hand in hand.

Maybe Tad could fill him in. Might as well ask. Ryan couldn't get any angrier than she'd been a few minutes ago. Although he could see her point about not telling him, it still pissed him off. What the hell would he have done if anything had happened?

"How do you feel about your cousin working here?"

Tad spun around and Carter could tell that the question had thrown him. "Who? Ryan?"

"Unless you got another cousin running around."

"Nope." He crossed his arms over his chest, and Carter decided maybe the man wasn't really lanky after all. He had some bulk on him. "What exactly are you trying to insinuate?"

"Insinuate nothing. I want to know what you think about her working here."

Ryan stepped in front of Tad and glared at Carter. "I don't think it's any of your damn business. This is my job. If you can't handle it, then get the hell out."

Now wait a minute. Get the hell out of the trailer or get the hell out of her life? Because neither choice was going to happen. He shook his head. Her mouth dropped open.

"Not gonna happen, sweetheart."

"Sweetheart?" Tad asked at the same time Ryan gasped.

"Stay out of it, Tad." Ryan didn't bother glancing at her cousin, but kept her focus—the one shooting daggers—on Carter.

"You have the audacity to call me sweetheart after all you've said to me this morning?"

Her outrage had him raising his eyebrows. "Do you think the things I said were uncalled for?"

"What did he say to you?" Tad's voice took on a threatening tone.

"How would you feel if you'd just learned about me what I just learned about you?" Carter questioned, ignoring Tad's sudden defensive stance.

Ryan's mouth opened and closed. Her hands went to her hips.

"What the heck are we talking about?" Tad scratched his head and looked back and forth between them.

"Nothing," Ryan snapped at the same time Carter said, "Epilepsy."

"Ah." Tad's one word was filled with understanding. "She just tell you about that, did she?"

"No." Ryan appeared ready to stamp her foot in a mini tantrum.

So damn cute.

"Out, Tad." Ryan pointed to the door.

Tad's forehead wrinkled. "You told me to stay put." He turned to Carter. "How'd you know about her condition if she didn't tell you?"

"The bracelet."

"Right. I keep telling her it's stupid to keep it in the dark, but what do I know?"

"Move." She pushed him toward the exit.

Tad resisted. "For what it's worth, I don't think this is the best place for her either. Too dangerous. Look what happened to Eric." He shrugged. "Tom has other ideas though."

"If you don't shut up, I'm going to kick your ass." This time she shoved at Tad's back with both arms. The man didn't budge.

"Who's Eric?" Carter fumed. How many men did she have in her life, for God's sake?

"The foreman. He broke his leg last week in an accident. Pretty bad too. Coulda been her."

"But it wasn't me," Ryan growled. This time she succeeded in forcing Tad forward with the toe of her boot to the back of his knee. "Eric's accident was just that. A freak thing."

"And you don't think having a seizure on site will be considered a freak thing?" Tad said what Carter wanted to yell.

"Jesus H. Christ," she shouted. "You know as well as I do that I haven't had an episode in two years. It's why I'm allowed to drive. Do I operate the heavy machinery? No. Do I use the I-beams as my personal balance beam? No. Am I standing in the presence of the bright, flashing welder? No. So get the hell off my back. Tom trusts in my abilities or he wouldn't have put me here."

"No, he wouldn't have." Tad nodded in agreement. "He would have put me here."

"Exactly. So until I'm flopping around on the ground like you two seem to have me doing every five minutes the way you're talking, let me do my job. I went to school and worked my tail off the same as you, Tad. Give me a chance to prove I'm not going to let you down, would you?"

Crap. Shit. The woman knew how to make a man feel the size of a pea. Carter swallowed. He had to give her credit. She knew which buttons to push. Perhaps he wasn't being fair.

"Leave. Now." Ryan didn't lift her gaze from the floor. She looked dejected and it tore at Carter's heart to know he was responsible for dousing the light in her eyes.

"Fine. Going." Tad grudgingly walked to the door, yanked it open and disappeared, slapping the door shut behind him.

Carter followed Tad to make sure the man had really gone away. He needed the privacy for a few minutes.

"You too." Her voice was firm.

"What?" Carter pretended not to understand. No way was she going to throw him out now. Not before he'd groveled at her feet for forgiveness for being a total ass.

She sucked in a breath and finally raised her face to his. "You heard me. I have work to do."

"And I have other things in mind," Carter said, standing his ground.

"Are you kidding me? If you think for even one second I'm going to let you—"

He stepped over to her and grabbed her hands, holding tight when she tried to wiggle loose. "Forgive me."

He smiled at her confusion.

He would have to touch her, wouldn't he? Ryan fought her body's response to him. She would not give in. She would not be swayed by the heat shimmering in his eyes. She would not let the tingle in her clit rule her brain.

She would not, she would not, she would not.

"Forgive me?" He tilted her face up to his with a crooked finger under her chin.

His lips were so close. Close enough to kiss. Three inches max. She knew what they would taste like. Two inches. Slow motion. What the hell was he waiting for?

"For you to forgive me." He whispered the words.

Had she said that out loud? One inch. One more inch...

His lips landed on hers, soft when she would have sworn he was angry enough to take her with a vengeance. But who gave a crap how he kissed when all she wanted to do was strip her jeans off and crawl onto the rock-hard dick currently pressed against her belly.

Ryan opened to him, accepted his tongue in her mouth, tangled hers with his and lifted a leg to his hip. One large hand, calloused she knew, gripped her ass check, squeezing. His fingertips grazed her pussy through thick denim and she wanted to cry out at the almost-nonexistent touch. It wasn't enough. She wiggled in his hold, trying to get closer when his feet started moving them backward.

His lips traveled away from her mouth, across her jaw and to her ear. "Does this mean I'm forgiven?"

The velvet silk of his words sent a shiver through her body. If he didn't fuck her soon...

"Forgiven?" What had they been talking about?

"Mmm-hmm. For being a jerk. Though I'm not sure whether to paddle your ass for worrying me or just fuck you into submission."

Her butt hit the desk behind her as his teeth raked along her neck. "I don't care which." She gasped and jerked her head up so fast she nailed his nose with her forehead. "I didn't say that."

A wicked grin transformed his face. "You did." With both hands on her hips, he lifted her to sit on the desk, spread her thighs and situated himself between them. Then he paused, his eyes creasing as if in thought.

"Is it...safe?"

The man was a puzzle. "Is what safe?"

Carter sighed and took her cheek in one palm. "To, you know, have sex."

"Oh my God." She would have jumped off the table but he had her pinned so she opted for slapping him instead. The blow, meant to be harsh, was. It cracked against his shoulder, making him wince. "You are an unbelievable bastard, you know that? We've been going at each other for two weeks. Has anything happened? No. I hardly think you knowing about it is likely to cause me to go into spasms."

"I seem to recall many times I've caused you to spasm." He brushed a fingertip over one of her nipples straining against her shirt, and she sucked in a breath.

"Exactly. The good kind of spasms." She groped for the tails of his shirt and pulled them free from his pants so she could feel the softness of his satiny skin. Her palms traced a path up his sides, lifting his shirt until she reached his pecs.

"Turnabout is fair play." He stepped back out of her reach and stripped the T-shirt off her torso before she could take another breath, then stared at her chest.

If she were at all self-conscious, she would cover herself from his gaze. Instead she arched her back and did her small breasts proud. "Not thinking about epilepsy now, are you?"

"Don't be a smart ass, sweetheart." He moved in again and pushed the straps of her bra off her shoulders to reveal pert nipples. With a flick of his thumb and forefinger he undid the clasp between her breasts. "I never get tired of looking at you."

"You're not so bad yourself." She wanted to tear through the buttons of his shirt but tackled them one by one, exposing his abs inch by tan inch. He had a tickle spot right below his left armpit which she found without error.

He jerked in response and reached for her wandering fingers. "Not this time."

"What?"

"The innocent card won't fly."

She pouted and fluttered her lashes.

"That won't work either."

"Why I just don't know what you're referring to, Carter," she cooed in her best *Gone with the Wind* imitation.

He grunted and left her sitting there, boobs hanging out— as much as it was possible for little boobs to hang—and her clit ringing with need.

"Hey. Where are you going? I wasn't done yet."

He turned and walked backward, looking devilishly sexy with his shirt open to the top button and red tie swinging over his naked chest, pointing at her reward.

"You want Tad to walk in on us?"

Ryan's cheeks heated. She'd been ready to have sex on her desk without once thinking about the fact that anyone could have walked in. First day on the job and she'd get caught screwing around. Literally. The thought had her leaping from the desktop.

"Right. We can't do this."

"The hell we can't." The lock clicked decisively with a flick of his wrist, and Ryan licked her lips.

Jeez the man had some kind of effect on her libido, making her forget everything except wanting to partake of his body. If the gleam in his eye meant anything, he didn't have any qualms about fucking her on her desk.

She noticed her nipples and clit had no qualms either.

"Jeans down to your knees, bend over the desk."

"Excuse me?" Her heart raced. She'd never heard that particular tone from his mouth before and couldn't decide if it scared her or excited her.

"You heard me."

He tugged on his tie, loosening the red silk enough to slip it over his head. Wouldn't want to retie it now would he? He pulled it off and tossed it somewhere behind him. With one hand, he unbuttoned the last remaining button and with the other, unbuckled the black belt threaded through his khakis. Watching as he stalked her from across the small trailer, Ryan swallowed. The next thing to go was the zipper on his pants, revealing blue plaid boxers, his cock a hard ridge straining to escape, the broad, smooth head poking out from the opening.

She was so going to get fired.

Chapter Four

He wanted to smile at the unsure look that crossed her beautiful features. Her blue eyes sparkled with a mixture of uncertainty and desire and her bra clung to her elbows where it had fallen earlier. A beautiful flush stole over her chest, telling him the one thing he needed to know.

She wanted to be naughty. Her eyes flashed to the door at his rear. Making sure he'd locked it?

Carter decided to give her another chance to do his bidding before he did it for her. "Jeans down, bend over, sweetheart."

That pink tongue of hers darted out again to moisten her lips, and if her nipples could speak, they'd be screaming, "Take me, take me!"

Eyes wide as he divested himself of his shirt, she shrugged out of the bra and reached for her fly. Then her chin lifted and she caught his gaze as if in challenge. She quickly yanked the denim to her knees. Red panties flaunted themselves, practically taunting him to remove them from her slender legs and stuff them in his pocket as a memento for later. He may have to do just that.

He twirled his finger in the air, waiting not quite so patiently for her to finish what he'd requested of her.

"You will pay for this," she mumbled, turning to face the desk before slowly and provocatively bending at the waist. Ryan glanced over her shoulder at him, her lips pursed, nostrils flared.

She definitely wanted this.

The jeans prevented her legs from spreading and provided him with a gorgeous view of her ass. He'd take her there someday, he decided, show her how he could make her feel the bite of painful pleasure.

As it was, she wiggled the delectable cheeks of her bottom, tempting him at a time when she shouldn't be messing with him. Didn't she realize how nervous she made him now? How he wouldn't be able to work without wondering if she was all right. He envisioned a long night of research to find out exactly what he was dealing with.

Drawing his cock out for her to see, Carter stroked himself. "I'm going to take you from behind, sweetheart. The way you're standing there, there won't be much you can do to stop me. It'll be tight between your thighs. Will feel so good with you squeezing me. Then when I'm deep inside you, stroking your channel until you beg for it, I'm going to spank your ass."

Ryan's burst of confidence seemed to slip. He touched a rounded butt cheek with the weeping head of his cock, spreading pre-come over the soft skin. She shivered, and her eyes closed and her teeth came out to bite her lower lip.

Carter dug in his back pocket for the condom stored in his wallet. He dropped the leather to the ground, tore the packet with his teeth and rolled the rubber over his erection. Teasing the taut ring of her anus with one hand, he pressed the other between her shoulder blades and urged her further over the desk.

"Grab the other side and don't let go." He traced the length of her spine as she complied with what appeared to be nervous fingers. Following the line of her hip around to her belly, Carter wedged his free hand into the space between her thighs and sought the bundle of nerves hidden there. He knew he'd found it when Ryan bucked with a squeak.

"Shh," he soothed, lining his cock up with her vagina. By the slickness gathered at her clit, he could tell she was ready to take him.

Ryan grunted at his initial penetration, contracting her muscles against his length as he tried to push in. The entry was like nothing he'd ever experienced before. He watched his cock disappear into her sheath and for the first time wondered what it would be like not to wear a condom. He wanted to feel the slick, wet heat of her body as he thrust inside her, wanted to spill his seed inside her womb.

Carter shook his head. A glance up her torso and down her outstretched arms showed white knuckles gripping the edge. She liked the position just as much as he did.

Her inner walls clutched his dick, threatening to cause him to come with the first lunge as if he were seventeen not thirty-eight. She wiggled her ass, making things worse for him. A drop of sweat trickled off his forehead. Son of a bitch. He had to grit his teeth to keep from going at her. But then the pale skin of her bottom glared up at him, fairly begging for his hand to turn it pink. If she thought to entice him, to get him to move before he was ready, he would just have to punish her. He'd threatened to already, why not make good on it?

He brought his left hand down on the smooth, creamy pad of flesh with a thwack.

Ryan took offense, but holy shit the immediate response of her pussy on his dick was more than enough to make up for her initial incense.

"What the shit? You said I'd be begging for you to spank me." She glared at him over her shoulder. "There weren't no beggin' goin' on, mister."

In response, Carter grinned, sucked his thumb into his mouth and pressed the wet digit into her anus to the first knuckle. Leaving her clit for the moment, he smacked her again.

Her head hit the desktop with a thunk, and if her butt hadn't constricted around him, he might have believed her indignation. She liked it.

Carter withdrew his cock and heard her swift intake of breath.

She groaned and rolled her head back and forth. "Shit. Anytime you're ready, bucko."

"Is that begging I hear?"

"Just move, you cocky bastard."

"I like cocky." He swiveled his hips and Ryan's back arched.

Her fingers fisted and one hand left the edge to lift in menace. He swatted her behind again, his eyeballs rolling when the action had direct impact on his dick. Perhaps he'd just discovered a way to fuck without ever moving.

"Put the hand down."

She lifted it higher.

His hand hovered over her butt. "I can stand here all day, my partner's wife is having a baby so there's no one to answer to back at the office. You, however, will probably have need of this trailer, especially if your father is coming."

"Shit."

"I believe you said that already," he said, mocking her with the words she'd thrown at him last night.

The hand slowly lowered and curled over the edge once more. He had to move. Not that he had a choice. His balls were drawn up impossibly tight and his eyes were crossed. He was likely to pass out from pleasure sooner rather than later.

"Jesus. Move." Her bark had the right affect.

Carter withdrew his thumb from her hole so he could grab her hip for leverage. The finger at her clit slipped and slid in a circle on the tiny bead.

Then he moved. In and out of the precious woman who'd somehow managed to possess his mind and heart with her smile and wit and now her vulnerability. His balls slapped against her and it was only then he realized that in the fog of lust he hadn't even taken his own pants off. Talk about a quickie on the boss's desk.

The fire built inside him, sizzling a pathway down his spine. Ryan stiffened beneath him, her back undulating. He felt the coil of her climax ready to strike.

"Don't stop."

As if he could. "Nope."

He hammered into her, working toward wringing every ounce of orgasm he could get from both of them. She straightened and Carter caught her with an arm around her waist. Her hand seized his where it met her sex, grinding his fingers into her clit.

With a shout, Carter slammed his cock deep and held her back to his chest. Wave after wave of come spilled into the condom.

"No, no." She shook her head, her words almost a sob. "Not done…"

Carter pressed on her clit using the friction of her own rotating hips to finish her off.

She came with a gasp of surrender, her clit throbbing under his fingertips, her body unbendable in his hold, and as he glanced down her torso he saw that her nipples were hard pebbles. He ached to take them in his mouth, to torture her further, but since he was no contortionist he'd have to lavish them with attention later.

Apart from the constant muted noise of the construction site outside, their heavy breathing was the only thing breaking the silence inside the trailer. Ryan reached for the back of his neck and raked her nails along the skin there.

Ryan sighed in the afterglow of good sex. Carter made her body sing in a way no other man ever had. He knew how to play, that was for sure.

He also had the ability to turn her brain to mush with one look. She had a feeling if he said *drop to your knees and suck my cock right now*, she'd do it. And lap it up like it was her last meal on Earth.

Carter plucked at a nipple and suddenly Ryan flashed into the present dimension. Surely she'd been in an alternate one for the past fifteen or twenty minutes. A shiver raced over her skin, leaving goose bumps in its wake. She dropped her hands to her sides, dislodging Carter's where it still played with her quivering clit.

It was a sad, ugly truth that she missed his touch when he wasn't around. After two weeks of their being together. What did that make her?

She looked over the desk she'd been ravished on. The normally pristine surface with its pencils and papers in their proper place was now completely discombobulated. It was a wonder she hadn't stabbed herself to death on one of the sharpened-to-a-pinpoint pencils.

"Umm...that was...wow."

"Yeah." His lips teased the side of her throat and down across her collarbone, and his hands smoothed up her abdomen to her breasts.

The phone rang, scaring the shit out of her. She leapt out of his arms, nearly falling to her face. Thank God she'd gotten her hands beneath her or she would have. Laughing, Carter helped her stand.

"This would be a whole lot easier if I'd taken the stupid things off, bucko."

"Maybe, but not nearly as fun."

"So says the man not on his hands and knees."

"Yet another position I'm going to take you in."

She swiped her bra off the floor before reaching for the phone. Damn thing wouldn't shut up.

"Ryan *Cooper*." She shot him a look to make sure he'd heard her name. He had and smiled while shrugging back into his shirt and buttoning the thing. What a shame to cover up such a god-like set of abs. The construction business had done him well.

"Is he in yet?" the gruff voice on the other end of the line asked.

"Who?" Ryan searched for her shirt and yanked her jeans over her sore ass. She curled her lip in Carter's direction. The jerk smirked.

"Your cousin, Ryan. Is Tad in?"

"Tad?" Was Tad in? Was her brain in? The alternate dimension had really done a number on her. "Yes. Yes, I saw him a few minutes ago." Give or take twenty.

"I'm on my way. Are you okay? You sound a little stressed."

"No. Not stressed." Her ass stung like hell, but stressed? No, she could honestly say she'd had the stress fucked right out of her.

"Things are running smoothly then?"

"Tom. It's only been three hours since I arrived. Did you expect things to fall apart the second I stepped on the lot?"

"No, *I* didn't. I know what you're capable of. But your mother worries about you. She made me ask."

"Uh-huh." If it were up to her mother, Ryan would still be in a playpen with only her blankie to keep her company. Overprotective didn't even begin to describe Carol Dixon.

"Actually." She eyed Carter stuffing his parts back into his boxers and pants after discarding the spent condom in some tissue. "Carter Malone is standing in the trailer with me at this precise moment."

His head popped up and she stuck her tongue out at him.

"Carter Malone?"

"Yep."

"As in Carter Malone of Malone and Casey, Carter Malone."

"Yes, Tom. The Carter Malone." Was she in a déjà vu or what? Tom seemed as surprised as she had. Of course, her stepfather hadn't been sleeping with the architect for the last two weeks.

"Great. Make him stay there too. I should probably talk to him at the same time."

The grim tone in his voice snagged her attention away from where she stared, transfixed, as Carter put his tie back on.

"Tom?"

"I'll explain everything when I get there. Trust me. Ten minutes. Bye."

The line disconnected before she could get a word in edgewise. What in the world?

"Something wrong?" Carter retrieved the phone from her hand and placed it on the table then proceeded to dress her like he would a toddler. Bra on, clasped in front, tugging to make sure her breasts were snuggled correctly, shirt over her head, arms in the holes, jeans zipped and snapped. All while she stood wondering what was going on with Tom. It wasn't like him to be secretive.

"I'm not sure. But my stepfather has requested to meet you. He'll be here in ten."

Ten minutes. Or less, more likely. And damn. They'd fucked on her desk. Anyone walking in would know exactly what they'd done. The area screamed, "I got fucked on my desk and lived to tell about it." Complete with sweaty body imprint across the top.

"Ten minutes," she whispered.

Reading her thoughts, Carter swung into action. He collected the papers and stacked them while Ryan grabbed for the rogue pencils and dumped them back in their holder. One set of blueprints had hit the floor, come unrolled and lay curled at the base of the desk. Carter dealt with it. Ryan snagged the lamp from the floor and set it upright.

Had they really done that much thrashing around?

"Is that it?" She turned in an arc, sweeping the room to make sure they'd gotten rid of all the evidence. Everything except the scent of sex that permeated the space. She snapped her fingers. "Bless the last foreman and his bizarre need for air fresheners." She remembered seeing them in the drawer where she'd stashed her clothes and grabbed one.

"I think we've hidden all the evidence, sweetheart." Carter leaned a hip against the desk, and knocked over the pencils yet again. With a calm she was glad one of them felt, he reached back and picked them up.

She could only imagine what Tom would think if he found out she was sleeping with the architect. Damn it, she'd worked too hard to get to this position, no way would she screw things up now. Nor would she let Carter.

"I'd appreciate you not saying anything to Tom about this."

One eyebrow rose. "About this? Or about us?"

"Both."

The other one lifted to meet the first. "Are you ashamed of me, Ryan? I am totally insulted." He put a hand over his heart and tried to look wounded.

Ryan snorted.

"Not right now at least, okay?" She could handle them telling Tom someday. Like maybe five years after the project was finished, but not today.

"Will he think me not good enough for you?" He clasped her hand in his and entwined their fingers. Probably to keep her from smacking him again.

"It's not that." The man was exasperating.

"I know, I know. You worked very hard to get here and you don't want me to ruin it for you. I get it." He zipped his lips shut. "Not one word."

How in the hell had he gotten that from her? She stared at him, not sure what to say.

"I can read you like an open book."

The doorknob rattled behind her and she whipped her head around to look. Why didn't he come in? The knock on the door clued her in.

"We forgot to unlock it. Damn it." She stormed over to the door, her face on fire. If their quick tidy-up job didn't do the trick, having a locked door sure the hell would.

Tom's hand lifted to knock again just as she opened it. His eyes narrowed and she knew she'd been busted.

"Why is the door locked?" Tom stepped into the trailer.

"My fault entirely, sir." Carter crossed the room and offered his hand to her stepfather who took it immediately and gave it three generous pumps. "I'm afraid it's become habit since our office was robbed a couple years back. Have no idea why I still lock doors behind me. You'll have to excuse me."

Ryan held her breath at the not-quite-white lie. As explanations went, that one was pretty good. Tom took Carter in, clearly trying to decide whether or not to believe him and then nodded.

"Had a run-in with burglars a time back myself. I can totally understand."

Holy crap. He'd bought it. Ryan was shoved from the back.

"Move outta the way, cuz." Tad pushed past them all and headed for one of the two chairs in the trailer then dropped into one. "So what's up, Uncle Tom?"

Apparently Ryan wasn't the only person curious about Tom's strange attitude.

Tom sighed and put his hands on his hips. "I've just been with Eric, our last foreman," he said for Carter's benefit. "He claims what happened to him wasn't an accident."

Chapter Five

Carter's entire being went on alert. "What do you mean, it wasn't an accident?"

"Eric slipped while walking on a beam ten feet up. The slip was an accident, sure, but the fact that his harness failed to hold him was not. The material had been cut and since I know Eric is fastidious about checking his equipment every day, I know he would never have used a defective lifeline. He's one of the best foremen I have."

Carter nodded. Not many men would. Only those with a death wish and deep-rooted hatred of OSHA.

"Anyway. Eric said he'd left his harness in the back of his truck when he went to lunch and that it looked the same when he got back. Since he'd already checked it in the morning he didn't think he needed to a second time."

"Seems normal." Carter leaned back on the desk and rolled his eyes at the clatter of the pencils behind him.

"Jesus, Malone. How many times you gonna knock that over?" Ryan stomped over and cleaned up the mess, otherwise you could have heard a pin drop in the silence.

It wasn't until she finished and looked up that she realized everyone was looking at her. Carter smiled at the way her cheeks reddened.

"What? Damn things have been on the floor this morning more than they've been in the holder."

"I'm concerned about you working here now, Ryan. As is your mother." Tom put his hands on her shoulders.

Carter itched to take his place. Tom wasn't the only one concerned. If there were *accidents* on site, he didn't want Ryan in the crosshairs. Especially if it hadn't been Eric-the-man who'd been targeted but Eric-the-foreman. A title which Ryan now held.

"As am I." Carter crossed his arms over his chest. She had the ability to make him wilt but on this he would stand strong.

"Oh come on. Maybe someone here hated Eric. You know as well as I do he had his enemies. He could be a dick."

"This is true," interjected Tad, who'd been quiet until then.

"Okay so someone had it out for him. Let's not ask for trouble."

Carter wanted to grind his teeth at her seemingly nonchalant attitude. Someone had cut the fucking lifeline of the last foreman and she wanted to push it under the rug. To him, cutting a lifeline might as well be called attempted murder.

He held his tongue and spoke to her stepfather instead. "I'll have my security team look into this, Tom. I appreciate you including me in this."

Tom shrugged. "You would have found out about it sooner or later. I'm sure Eric will be pressing charges when the culprit is found."

"As well he should." Carter threaded his fingers through his hair. "Until then, count on there being at least some kind of security on site to keep an eye on things. Max Jensen is good. I'll see if he's available."

"Hello, I am the foreman now. Don't I have any say in the matter?"

"Stubborn, stubborn girl." Tom shook his head and hugged her to him. "We all know how hard you worked to get this. No one's going to take away your shot."

That's what she was afraid of. Someone seeing her weakness and trying to oust her for it. When she was more qualified than most men for the job. But in a *man's* world she now had two things against her. Boobs and epilepsy.

Ryan blew out a breath. "The last thing we need is some bystander getting hurt, Tom." She was trying her best to win her case but from the sound of things she was going to lose no matter what. Damn men thinking they were always doing what was best for her.

Carter bit his lip and looked down at the floor. She could tell he was trying not to smile. Since he didn't know how much she wanted this job, she'd give him a tiny bit of slack, but if he didn't get it through his thick skull pretty damn quick that she wasn't going to back down, she was going to have to brain him. He wouldn't look so high and mighty flat on his ass would he?

Then again, she knew exactly how he looked flat on his ass. Of course, he'd been naked at the time, which made the view so much nicer.

"I'll keep an eye on her too." Tad's words almost made Ryan groan.

She gritted her teeth. "I don't need a keeper."

Tad snorted. "You've needed one since you were born."

Ryan turned on him, ready to punch him in the eye. Wouldn't be the first time the two of them had gone a few rounds. They'd spent a ton of time together growing up because their fathers had been so close. Although Tom wasn't her biological father, he'd stepped up to the plate when she was still a baby. Tom's brother, her step-uncle, Chris, had been part of her life from the beginning, and no one had ever treated her like an outsider. Except for the epilepsy. The men in her family were definitely an overprotective lot and to this day still tended to coddle her.

All except Tad who did his best to antagonize the shit out of her.

"Children." Tom stepped between them. "It wouldn't matter

if you were a man, Ryan. The truth is someone sabotaged Eric's equipment. If it could happen to him, it could happen to anyone. Especially a more vulnerable target. Got it?"

Tom had a fairly decent way of blowing the wind right out of her sails. He was correct. She did make a more vulnerable target. She was grown up enough now to admit her faults.

"Fine, Carter. Send your babysitters."

"I will." The way Carter said so made her think the alternative had never been in question.

She scowled at him, despite how it made her feel petty and childish. "Don't you have work to do?"

Tom cleared his throat. "We do work for Mr. Malone, Ryan."

"I have a feeling he's gone beyond *Mr. Malone* with her." Tad stood, a wicked gleam in his eye, and Ryan couldn't resist. She stomped on his toe with the heel of her boot.

The desired effect was not forthcoming. Instead he laughed, pulled her into the crook of his arm and proceeded to give her a noogie. Fucking humiliating her in front of her *boss*. She decided she would maim her cousin later when there were no witnesses.

"Ryan?" Tom was eyeing both her and Carter dubiously.

When she finally managed to break free of the schmuck's hold, she found herself being stared down by the older man.

"We didn't know who we were." Yeah, that sounded coherent.

"Sir." Carter lifted his hand for another shake from Tom. "Your daughter and I have been seeing each other for a couple of weeks now. It wasn't until this morning that we discovered the work connection."

The statement made Tom's eyes widen. "Seeing each other?"

"Yes, sir."

"Guess you know why the door was locked now, huh, Uncle Tom?" Tad danced out of the way of Ryan's reach.

"I guess so." Her stepdad smiled and she wondered about it before turning her quickly-rising-to-the-boiling-point anger at Tad.

"Asshole."

"Get lost, nephew, before I let her loose to destruct you piece by piece."

"As if," Tad murmured, heading out the door.

"So. You're seeing someone?"

"Oh my God." How on Earth could the man do this to her? Hello? Was she still in high school?

"Your mother will be pleased."

"I'll bet." She wished the floor would swallow her up.

"I expect you to call her."

"She will." Carter gripped her hand, threading her fingers through his. "I'll make sure."

Tom's smile nearly blinded her. The man was in heaven. Thankful no doubt that he could report back to her mother that all was well in Ryansville and by golly, the girl had even gone and gotten herself a man. She wondered if he would tell her mother that she'd fucked said man on her desk too.

Ryan knew she should go ahead and X out this Sunday afternoon because it was a sure bet her mother would call her before noon today and invite them for Sunday brunch. A brunch that would include a grilling of momentous proportions, and she wasn't talking barbecue.

The men were finally gone, off to inspect the site. It had taken Ryan promising she would talk *and* listen to Max Jensen the super-spy PI-guy whatever-he-was to make Carter go. She wiped a hand over her face and slumped in her chair. What a damn morning. She'd come to work pumped to do the job her stepfather had entrusted her to do, fought with then fucked her lover of two weeks, been caught by her family after having engaged in such an act and now here she sat waiting on some security hero to come and save the day. Like she was a girl.

"God save me from men." She groaned and laid her head on the desk. If she didn't know it would hurt like hell, she'd bang it a few times to clear her head. And since her head was already pounding...

Or was that the door? "Ms. Cooper?" Her eyes narrowed at the gruff male voice on the other side of it.

She wasn't done being a baby. A little more alone time would have been nice. Ryan yanked open the door to find a stranger. Her heart thumped.

"I'm Max Jensen, ma'am."

Sheesh. All their freaking warnings. She was losing her mind. Since when had a stranger thrown her for a loop? Especially one as good-looking as this one. He epitomized yum. Lots of muscles, military-short cropped hair, tall, tan, green eyes...

Hello, you have a man already. Doesn't the smell of sex shrouded with floral air freshener in an enclosed space remind you of that fact?

"Ma'am?"

"Ugh." She would kill Carter later for tying her all in a knot. "Come in."

His face brightened with a hundred-watt smile. He must have women hanging all over him. Somewhere out in the world were no doubt a whole bunch of drooling females. "What can I do for you, Mr. Jensen?"

"Max, please. Carter sent me to check into some things. Just wanted you to know I was here in case you saw me out there wandering around and wondered who the hell I was."

"Right." She could only imagine. Good thing most of the construction crew were men. Otherwise the project would come to a standstill while Max made his inquiries. The few women they did have were sure to take up a good portion of his time just so they could keep looking at him. On the other hand, there were two or three gay men on the payroll. Perhaps she should warn him?

He pushed his hands into his pockets. The action revealed the butt end of a nasty-looking gun at his hip.

"Are you planning on shooting someone?"

He smiled again. "Nope. But I don't leave my house without it. I've had it for so long it's kind of an extra appendage. Besides, if someone points a nail gun at me, I want to be prepared."

"Uh-huh. Mr. Jensen, if any one of my workers points a nail gun at you for any reason other than to protect themselves from your weapon, then they'll be fired on the spot."

"Then I can use it to help escort them from the lot, yeah?"

"Whatever floats your boat. Can I get you anything to drink? There's water, coffee, a few sodas left over from Eric..." She turned and retrieved her decaf pitcher from its maker and poured herself a cup.

"That looks great, thanks."

"Oh no, this one is mine. Decaf. Sorry. Me no share." She took a long sip, loving the warm, chocolate-tasting feel of it sliding down her throat and moaned.

Max laughed. "Does the caffeine mess with your epilepsy?"

She narrowed her eyes. "How did you know about that already?"

"You're dating Carter. He's a very protective sort of man. Always handles his women with care. But even if he hadn't told me, I'd have dug into your background and found it before I got here."

If her eyes were any narrower she wouldn't be able to see anymore. "Great. I'm so glad it's so easy. By the way, that kind of shit could get him dumped real quick."

Those pearly whites showed themselves again. The man must have permanent laugh lines in his face. "I don't think you can get rid of him quite that easily."

"How would you know? You slept with him too?"

He snorted. "Hell no. He's not my type."

"What? Egotistical, overbearing, know-it-all doesn't do it for you?"

"No, but apparently he does it for you."

"What can I say?" She poured him a cup from the regular coffee pot and handed it to him before drinking from her own again. She was a sucker for the brown-eyed blondie. Carter revved her engine so to speak. And until this morning when he'd weirded out about her epilepsy, things had been going along so smoothly.

Even though he'd freaked, like she knew he would, Ryan didn't want to lose him.

The man fucked you on your desk post news, idiot. He didn't look ready to fuck and run either. Not to mention he told Tom outright that you were dating.

"So you never answered the question. Does caffeine screw with your epilepsy?"

Ryan took a long, hot swallow before answering. She hated people prying into her personal life. Made her feel like a bug under a microscope, and since she'd spent the majority of her childhood that way, she was going to live her adult life the way she wanted to. Not the way anyone else did.

However, the truth wasn't going to hurt here. Max needed to know anything pertinent to investigate what was happening at the site, and if she was going to be a so-called target, then she might as well divulge.

"Yes it does. Along with a few other things. Flashing lights, migraines, certain medicines, sex."

Max spewed the mouthful of coffee he'd sipped, choking and coughing until the spasms subsided.

"Just kidding."

"Good one." He wiped up his mess with a tissue from the

desk and tossed it in the trash.

"I take it though, from the fact you drive and work here, that it's under control."

"Yes. Haven't had a seizure in two years. I'm very careful, Mr...Max. I think you'll find that what happened to Eric is someone taking their vengeance out on a man who, although he did a fantastic job as foreman, wasn't the most personable man in the world. I'm sure this has nothing to do with this particular job but Eric himself."

Max nodded and set his half-empty coffee cup down. "Maybe. I still have to look into all angles. Whether or not it was Eric who was targeted, or the leadership, someone caused another man to fall and get injured."

"And for that he...or she, should pay. I'll stand behind you one hundred percent either way."

"All right then. Mind showing me around?"

"Nope." Ryan grabbed her jacket from the coat tree in the corner and shrugged into it.

"Any ideas on who might have hated Eric enough to want to do him harm? Cutting a man's safety harness isn't really a prank. There's no way to know when the harness would fail. Eric could have been four stories up, not ten feet."

Ryan locked the door behind them. "I know." When she turned and surveyed the site, she saw Carter and Tom hovering over the plans. Carter held a hammer in both hands and he was...caressing it almost. She smiled. It was obvious he wanted to dive in and help out with the building portion of construction. The way he stared at the steel beams in front of him made her think of a little boy in front of the most rad BMX bike in the world. One he wasn't allowed to touch.

Her knee buckled when she stepped toward him.

"Whoa." Max grasped her elbow to keep her from going down. "You all right?"

"Yeah. Musta stepped on something." She turned in a circle

to search the ground. There wasn't anything that would have made her stumble.

"No harm no foul. Carter's watching you, better not do that again." He chuckled and let go.

"Yeah." Her knees both felt shaky now. As did her hands. What the hell?

She straightened, a sudden thought smacking her between the eyes, and searched for the aura that always, without fail, preceded one of her seizures. Panic stole over her. She hadn't had one in so long! Had she conjured one simply by talking about it so much this morning? Would she never be free of the stigma? Taking a deep breath, she searched inward for the aura. It was nowhere to be found. So no seizure. Going from warmth to chill? Getting up too fast? Come to think of it, her head *was* a little swimmy.

"Are you sure you're okay?" The concern in Max's voice jerked her out of her musings.

"Yes. I'm sure. Guess the cold got to me."

His concerned lightened. "You're one of those people who are always cold even if it's warm, aren't you?"

"No." Why was he asking stupid questions? They were halfway across to the area where Carter and Tom stood when another wave of dizziness hit her. She stumbled again.

"Shit." She heard Max from a distance and then a shout. Strong arms caught her around her waist and the world spun. Blue sky greeted her as she opened her eyes.

"What happened?" She was so tired. And... "Cold."

"Get a blanket," Max barked, hurting her ears.

Heavy warmth ensconced her, fighting to win over the nausea stirring in her belly.

"Ryan. Ryan." Carter was there above her, frantically peering down at her, his face a war of confusion and worry.

"What?" They needed to give her some space, let her get up. She didn't want her men to see her this way. They might think

119

she couldn't handle the job. "Need to...get up." She pushed on whatever held her down to no avail. It held her tight like a heavy weight settling on her chest. Her teeth chattered she was so cold.

"I called nine-one-one," someone said.

"Why?" There wasn't anything wrong. She'd tripped, for God's sake, and they were treating her as if she were made of spun glass. A pain shot through her stomach and for a second she thought she might vomit.

"Roll her on her side." Tom's voice soothed her. He knew how to handle things.

"Aren't you supposed to put something in her mouth?" she heard another voice ask.

God no, she thought to whoever had spoken. The last time someone had done that she'd practically bitten off her tongue *and* choked to death.

"No," Tom snapped.

"A seizure?" This from Carter. God he was seeing her at her best. If she hadn't run him off before, this would do the trick. She'd wake up later with no memory of what had happened and no Carter to comfort her. The mere thought was enough to make her puke even if she hadn't already been feeling sick.

The shaking started in her right leg and moved across her hips and up her side. Her teeth slammed together, her spine arched sharply. She felt it all, begged it to go away and leave her alone. Except something was wrong. Different. This was not one of her seizures. She had to tell them. But the voices were drowning her out. The yelling, the sirens, the constant banging. How could she get a word in edgewise? Her brain was sluggish, not allowing her thoughts to coalesce into words, and the noise wouldn't shut up.

Tom would never let her back on the site again.

Chapter Six

Jesus Christ he'd never been so scared in his entire life. It was a scene he never wanted to see again for as long as he lived. One minute he'd been watching her progress toward him, the next her legs had buckled and she'd fallen to the ground. Thank God Max had been there to soften the impact. He'd managed to catch her before her face kissed the earth.

How had she lived like this?

Carter flipped an errant clump of hair from Ryan's forehead as he watched her rest. After being transported by ambulance to the hospital, doctors had stabilized her condition and given her a room to recover in. He'd been shocked when Tom told him her seizures didn't normally require any kind of medical intervention. They typically let the seizure run its course and offered comfort when it was over. This one had been different from normal.

As if epilepsy could ever be considered normal.

He didn't care if it was normal or not, seeing her eyes roll back in her head had nearly made him piss himself.

Tonight, while he watched her sleep—because he for damn sure wouldn't leave her side—he'd bone up on the disease and learn everything he could so he'd be ready for the next time.

As if things weren't bad enough, Tom had told him her driver's license would likely be stripped and worse, he wasn't sure how he could keep her as foreman. The reason he'd taken a chance was because she'd gone so long without an episode.

Tom had given him a little background on Ryan's seizures since Carter knew less than nothing. They had always followed a certain pattern. She'd see an aura, which in essence warned her of an upcoming seizure, she would zone out for a short time period and then the seizure would begin. Normally by that point they would've already gotten her to the ground, or she would have done it herself. Never had one come on so suddenly.

The doctors weren't clear as to why her symptoms had changed, but they'd done a series of blood work and were waiting on the results. For now, Tom had left Carter to wait for Ryan to wake up while he drove home to pick up Carol, her mother, who was frantic wondering what was happening. Carter was glad that Tom had talked her into not driving while she was in such a state or she'd likely be occupying the bed next to Ryan's.

The door opened behind him and Carter stood, eager to hear what the doctor had to say.

"How's she doing?" The doctor wasn't someone Carter recognized from the emergency room.

"I have no idea." No clue whatsoever. He wondered if he really knew anything about anything at the moment. Carter slipped his hands in his back pockets and waited while the doctor read Ryan's chart. After a few minutes and couple of nods the man looked up.

"I'm Doctor Kinney. I presume you're the fiancé, Carter?"

What the shit? Fiancé? He shook hands with the doctor's outstretched one.

"Yes I am." He might be surprised as hell, but he wasn't stupid. He wasn't family. Carter was going to owe Tom some huge favors. If he hadn't told Dr. Kinney that he and Ryan were engaged, then the most likely scenario would have been the doc giving Carter the brush-off based on privacy laws.

"I talked to her father a few minutes ago. He said you'd likely be here until Ryan went home." Kinney laid her chart at the foot of her bed and moved to the side. "So here's the deal.

While I'm sure, based on what the paramedics and Tom all said, that Ryan had a seizure, I'm not convinced it had anything to do with her epilepsy."

"What?"

"Yep." Kinney grabbed Ryan's wrist and checked her pulse, then whipped out a penlight and searched her eyes. "I suspect something other than the epilepsy caused her to have a seizure."

"What?" This time Carter shouted. Ryan never stirred. He scooped up her hand and held it tight. The fucking thing with Eric had nothing to do with Eric but was instead someone after the foreman. Apparently it didn't matter to their asshole suspect who he hurt, male or female. Carter yanked his phone out of his pocket and flipped it open, thumb poised to contact Max and give him the heads up.

"She came in with a low body temperature. Epilepsy does not cause a drop in temp. Her breathing was labored, thus the oxygen, again not a sign she's ever shown before. Her belly was tender, something she couldn't tell us while unconscious, but her body could. And she vomited twice in the ER. While vomiting can occur with some patients, again, that's not a symptom typical to Ryan. So unless her epilepsy has changed over the last couple of years and is manifesting itself differently, I'd have to say something else was at fault."

Carter was sick to his stomach. Had someone deliberately drugged Ryan in order to cause her to have a seizure? "I have security on the site right now. I'll have him look into it." He lifted the phone and punched the speed dial for Max, who was discussing the harness situation with the police who'd stayed at the site after Ryan collapsed.

"You do that. In the meantime, her vitals have stabilized for now and it should only be a matter of time before she wakes up. I know it sometimes takes hours for her to rouse after a normal seizure. There's no way to tell how long it'll be if this was drug induced."

"Yeah, Max, hang a sec, would you?" Carter took the phone from his ear. "Can't you find whatever it is in her blood?"

Kinney shook his head. "Sadly, no. There are any number of things out there that might cause a seizure, including something as simple as flashing lights. Regardless, the labs aren't always equipped to pick up trace amounts of a foreign substance. If she'd taken in a large amount, then maybe, but we didn't find anything in her blood workup today.

"Now, if you'll excuse me, I have a few other patients to see. I'll be back in to check on her later."

"Okay. Thank you for letting me know."

"You'll pass it along to Tom and Carol? They'll be worried."

"Yes."

The door clicked shut behind the doctor, leaving Carter alone in the room. He stroked Ryan's arm then heard Max saying, "Hello?"

"Max, I'm here."

"They think she was drugged?"

"He does. I'm guessing I don't even need to tell you what to do."

"Hell no. I'm on it. See if you can get anything from her when she wakes up and give me a call. Did she see anything suspicious, talk to anyone she didn't know, drink something someone else gave her?"

"She was at work, Max, not a bar."

"Doesn't matter, people bring coffee and sweets to all kinds of jobs. Someone might have brought something in for her this morning. And I drank the same coffee and I didn't get... Son of a bitch."

Carter's heart thumped against his rib cage and the hair on the back of his neck stood up. "What?"

There was a rustling on the other end of the phone suggesting that Max was on the move. "I was going to say I drank the same coffee this morning that she did, but I didn't.

She wouldn't let me have any."

"Wouldn't let you?" Ryan didn't seem to Carter like the hard-ass type who didn't share.

"No. She said, my decaf, me no share. She gave me the regular from a different pot and slurped down the fake crap. So either she drank regular when she thought it was decaf or someone could have tampered with it. I'll let you know what I find."

Max disconnected before Carter could speak. He stared at the phone, his temper rising to the boiling point. If Max found one shred of evidence that Ryan's drink had been tampered with, Carter would hunt the bastard down who'd done it and not stop until the asshole was drawn and quartered.

There was cotton in her mouth and some weird shit blowing in her nose and tickling it. She felt hung over—or what she imagined hung over would feel like since she didn't ever drink. Random thoughts filtered through the fog along with whispered voices.

Ryan struggled to turn in the direction of the sound. Her head had to have been weighed down with lead for all the good it did her. Even her hands seemed tied down.

Was that her mother talking? What in the hell? And Tom and...Carter? Shit. Had she flaked out at Sunday brunch? Taken a nap? Where the heck was she?

She opened her eyes to a cloud of blur. Blinking them helped relieve the problem but left her facing a white ceiling.

"Mom?" Her voice croaked and she wasn't sure if anything had come out at all or if she only imagined speaking aloud.

"Oh, right here, honey." Her mother's face came into view. Then Tom's and Carter's. "You're going to be just fine."

"What happened?" She hoped one of them would fill her in because the strain of wondering was giving her a headache.

"You had a seizure." Her mother was crying. Damn. Ryan hated making her mother cry. Someone touched her leg, soothing her rapidly fraying nerves.

She'd been drinking coffee with...Max, right, super-spy-PI-guy Max. Then what? They'd gone outside so she could show him around. Tom and Carter had been there, watching the construction. Odd. She didn't normally remember shit about her episodes. *But this wasn't a normal episode.*

"Not a seizure." She yawned as the pressure of whatever had happened tried to drag her under again. Ryan caught her stepfather and Carter eyeing each other. They knew something.

"What do you mean, sweetheart?"

Ryan smiled. She loved when Carter called her sweetheart. No one else ever had.

"Wasn't the same. No aura. No warning," she murmured, letting the sleepiness invade.

"But it's been a long time since you had one. Perhaps they're changing?" Tom sounded sympathetic, which perked her up.

"No." No, she was certain whatever had occurred was not her epilepsy. "Not the same." She did her best to be adamant but had a feeling she came out more unsure than anything. "Knees were shaky, sick...lightheaded."

"Okay, okay, sweetheart." Carter's murmur calmed her a bit. "Just rest. Go back to sleep. I'll be here when you wake up. I promise."

She wanted to cry. She remembered now. Remembered worrying about him seeing her in the throes of a seizure and having him disappear on her. That when she finally woke up, he'd be gone instead of having his fingers laced with hers, comforting and not letting go.

Carter's frustration mounted. Ryan was too out of it to tell them anything more, like who might have wanted to drug her.

Tom laid a hand on Carter's shoulder. "We're going to go down to the cafeteria. You should come too."

"No. I want to be here when she wakes up again. I promised her I would be."

"Bless you. You're a good man." Tears pooled in Carol's eyes. She hugged him close, squeezing the breath out of him. "You'll be good for my daughter."

Yeah, if she'd keep him around long enough for him to show her how good he could be. Her epilepsy had made her gun shy, he knew, and he couldn't begin to think about how many times she might have been hurt in the past. Perhaps she'd never even tried for something permanent.

Carter had news for her. He wasn't going to go away so easily. She was stuck with him whether she wanted to be or not.

His phone rang. Carter glanced at the number before flipping it open and answering it. Jesus, he'd completely forgotten about Morgan and Ridge.

"Good news, I hope." He sure as hell needed some.

"It's a boy. Seven pounds four ounces, looks like his momma."

Carter sorta doubted that since from his recollection newborns tended to look more like shriveled-up pink raisins, but whatever. He was glad the baby was healthy. "Congratulations, man. How is momma?"

"She's good. Not sure she'll ever do this again, but she's holding him right now and happy as hell to have him out. We named him Brandon Michael. She's in room eight forty-two."

"I'll have to run up and see him in a few." Whenever Ryan woke up and he was sure she was fine.

"Run up?"

Oops. Figured his partner would catch on to the slip. "Uh, yeah. I'm here with Ryan."

"Who's Ryan?"

"Ryan Dixon to you, Ryan Cooper to me."

"I am so confused."

Carter smiled. "I've heard giving birth can do that to you."

"Malone."

"Ryan Dixon is the foreman you sent me to see today. Only he's not Ryan Dixon, *she's* Ryan Cooper, the woman I've been seeing. She works for her father. The previous foreman's accident wasn't an accident, we discovered, so I had Max come out to do some digging. But then Ryan had a seizure which had nothing to do with her epilepsy which I wasn't aware of her having, and now we're here in room six twelve while she recovers from a possible poisoning." How was that for a sixty-second rundown?

"What in the shit? I leave you to do one thing and all that happened?"

"Pretty much. It's really Morgan's fault, I think, because she's the one who normally keeps us altogether and sane."

"I'll tell her you said that." Ridge's voice was dry.

"You don't need to. I tell her every day." The phone beeped in his ear indicating another call. Max. "I gotta go, that's Max on the other line." He disconnected before Ridge could speak.

"Tell me you found something, Max," Carter said as his greeting.

"I did. You aren't going to like it though."

Carter's insides twisted. "Tell me."

"When I suspected the coffee, I returned to the trailer. Thought maybe I could send the pot of coffee off to the lab for testing. But when I got there someone else was already there throwing away the evidence."

"Who?" Carter gritted his teeth so hard he was sure they would crack. He wanted to punch someone. Ryan was laying here in bed, unable to defend herself, and the asshole who'd done this to her was wiping away his traces.

"Tad Dixon."

Carter exploded. "That son of a bitch."

"He denies having anything to do with either of the circumstances, but his answers were a little too smarmy for me so I let the police take over."

"Good." Here's to hoping the dick spent a great deal of time rotting in jail. "Let me know how it goes. I'll talk to Tom." He flipped the phone off and pocketed it.

Ryan twisted in her sleep with a moan, oblivious to the fact her cousin may have been the one to cause her grief. He grabbed her hand and sat next to the bed again.

Carter hadn't once suspected there was anything the least bit off about her cousin. Had anything Tad said earlier been a clue to his true feelings? He tried to recall. Tad had seemed quite the charmer to Carter at first. Easy to do, he guessed, while trying to hide the fact that you'd almost killed one man and were about to try and bring down your cousin. Christ, he'd been protective of her even, standing up for her during their conversation about the epilepsy.

Perhaps the only thing that might have been a clue was his stance on Eric. The job was dangerous, he'd said, "I don't think this is the best place for her either. Look what happened to Eric. Tom has other ideas though."

"Shit." Was that what this was all about? His need to be the foreman? Had Tad tried to knock off Eric, thinking he would replace him? Then gotten pissed enough to take out Ryan when she got the job instead of him?

Now he had to tell Tom his nephew was being questioned by the police for what would probably amount to attempted murder.

He punched in the number of Tom's cell and told the older man everything he'd learned and what he suspected. Tom was just as shocked as Carter had been. Not to mention hurt and angry as hell.

Chapter Seven

Ryan sank back in Carter's oversized tub and luxuriated in the feel of the warm bubbles swirling around her skin. She'd been released that morning from the hospital a day after her seizure, and no amount of talking had gotten Carter to let her out of his sight. Instead he'd brought her to his house and asked someone to go to hers and pick up a few things. She'd barely gotten him to leave her alone so she could chill out for a few minutes without him hovering.

Although she had to admit his form of hovering was much different than her family's version had been growing up. They tended to wrap her in a plastic bubble. She much preferred Carter's method of distraction—showering her with naughty kisses, and teasing the crap out of her until she was good and horny. There was definitely something to be said about horny. A girl could indubitably get used to it. And since she was spending the night...

God help Carter if he decided to go easy on her. The doctor had said she was fine after her run-in with Visine-laced coffee. The effects could have been worse. Much worse. Dead kind of worse. But she'd only had about a mug's worth of coffee the entire morning, what with Carter making her spill her first cup and Max disrupting the second in order to investigate. Those things combined prevented her from finishing her normal three-cup routine.

She really needed to shake the coffee anyway. It wasn't like the decaf was doing a damn thing for her.

Ryan still couldn't believe Tad had conspired to take out the foreman so he could have the job. When she'd finally woken up yesterday and Tom had been standing there so grief-stricken, she'd thought for a crazy moment they were going to tell her she had some incurable brain tumor or something.

What had come out of his mouth was the last thing she'd expected. Tad had been furious with Ryan's appointment to the job. Just when he'd thought he'd secured it by causing Eric to break his leg, Tom gave it to a girl. Naturally, her epilepsy had played right into his hands.

One small Google search later and Tad stupidly thought he could get rid of her by causing her to have a seizure. He was sure no one would allow her to stay if she was susceptible to her condition. The thought had never crossed his mind he might actually cause her death with eye drops. Apparently his Google search gave him only the bare minimum of facts.

She wondered if he liked men, since he was about to spend a few years surrounded by them. Even if she could forgive him for his lack in morality, Eric could not. He was ready to prosecute to the full extent of the law.

All because Tad felt with his dad's passing, he should have, by rights, been the foreman.

"Are you a prune yet?"

Ryan looked up at Carter's smiling face and smiled back. "Nope. I'm just getting nice and toasty."

"Are you hungry?"

She was hungry, but not for food. "What are you having?"

"That's a loaded question."

"So give me a loaded answer."

His eyes narrowed. "That would require me joining you."

"Then by all means..."

"Are you sure?"

Oh jeez, here it goes. The one thing she'd hoped wouldn't happen, for him to go all soft on her. "Either get in here or get out."

Carter leaned back in shock.

"I'm not going to break, Carter. I'm fine. Remember, the doctor said no restrictions? I'm sure sex is included in those directions."

"All right. Don't get your panties in a twist."

"If I were wearing any, that might be a problem, but since I'm not..."

She watched as he stripped to the skin, loving the play and ripple of tan skin over muscle. Scooting forward, she allowed him to sit behind her, his cock beautifully erect and ready for action. She'd never done it in the tub before. There was a time for everything, right? His fingers caressed her back, gently massaging the kinks. Perhaps she had been in the tub a bit too long.

Ryan relaxed into his chest and dropped her head on his shoulder. "God that feels good."

"I was worried about you," he admitted softly in her ear.

She sighed. "I know. I tend to have that effect on people. Everyone feels sorry for me."

"I didn't say I felt sorry for you." His arms came around her midsection, wrapping her in his own heat that had nothing to do with the warmth of the water. "You make it hard to feel sorry for you. What I said was, I was worried about you. There's a difference, see?"

She drew away and looked over her shoulder at him. "Do you think Tad's okay?"

"The man could have killed you. Why do you care?"

Ryan shrugged. "He had a moment of insanity. I'm not ready to forgive him for what he did, but he is still my cousin. I grew up with him. It's really hard to see what he's become."

Carter cupped her breasts in his palms and thumbed her

nipples, causing her to suck in a breath. "I know. I'm sure he's fine. He did make his bed after all."

"You're right."

"I'm always right." She heard the grin in his words.

"Oh yeah?" With his cock nestled at the small of her back it was getting hard to remember what they were talking about. All she knew was her need for him. She turned in his hold. "A little less talk?"

"And a lot more action."

"Please?"

He tapped her nose with a wet finger, traced it over her lips, down her chin and throat, then between her breasts before settling on the peak of one. "Begging already, sweetheart?"

"If it'll get me what I want." She would not be ashamed of how breathless she sounded. Her skin itched to have him drive inside her.

"Begging's not necessary right now. Later? Maybe. For now, I'm good with simple asking."

"Would you please fuck me?"

"No."

She was sure her eyes popped out of her head. Ryan came to her knees between his outstretched legs and crossed her arms over her chest. "Excuse me?"

"No fucking. Loving. I will make love to you." He gripped her hips and pulled her close to kiss her.

His tongue pushed into her mouth. It seemed like forever ago she'd kissed him, tasted him. She wanted to taste more of him but unless she wanted to drown, the act of swallowing his cock would have to wait until they were out of the water.

"Straddle me."

She did, putting her knees on either side of his thighs. His erection grazed her pussy and she nearly bent to impale herself on his length.

"Wait, sweetheart." His fingers found her pussy. Two of them slid into her while his thumb circled her clit.

"It's not enough, Carter. Please."

He kissed a nipple, sucking it into his mouth with a firm tongue. Little flames of desire licked across her skin.

"I'll take care of you." His murmured words barely penetrated the lust-filled fog controlling her mind.

She whipped her head up and stared at him. Surely he'd lost his mind. Here she was, craving his possession of her and he wanted to *take care* of her? While she'd normally love for him to take care of her, right now she wanted his cock inside her.

"No condom." He looked agonized.

"Oh. So what."

He grinned and scissored his fingers inside her, somehow nicking an ultra-sensitive spot, nearly causing her to jump.

"I hardly think you're ready for a baby, sweetheart, much as I'd love to see your belly round with my child."

"Pregnant?" How was she supposed to think with him doing what he was doing? She was lucky her eyes weren't crossed.

He added a third finger, stretching her wide, preparing her. "Yes, you know the thing that happens when a man leaves his sperm inside a woman?"

She smacked him, then bit her lip when he withdrew his fingers and stabbed them back in.

"Pill. I'm on the pill." Time to take matters into her own hands. Ryan lifted off his hand and settled herself where she wanted to be more than anything. She sank down on him, groaning in sync with Carter, whose eyes closed.

"You don't play fair."

"Nope. Never said I did." She moved on him, rising and falling until the water sloshed over the sides. She needed just a little more…

He added a thumb to the mix, zeroing in on her clit and

pushing her over the edge. She held herself rigid against his chest. Apparently he'd primed her well because she'd come but he hadn't.

"Sorry, sweetheart." He gripped her hips to hold her down and drove upward. Her clit throbbed with each thrust, prolonging her orgasm. Again and again he filled her. Just as she thought she might miraculously come again, Carter stiffened beneath her. Even through the heat of the water she felt him pour into her, and for the first time wondered what it would be like if she weren't on the pill. He'd opened her eyes to the possibility. Was that really what he wanted?

He must have sensed that she was close because instead of basking in his own glory he pressed a thumb to her clit once more. The cylinders were all still firing, sending an arrow of tingling sensation straight to her womb.

"Come for me one more time, Ryan."

She tried, sought the release sitting so close she could taste it. The kicker that sent her over the edge was his mouth on her nipple, his teeth biting gently on the nub and wringing the orgasm from her. Ryan arched into it, urging the throbbing pulse at her clit to keep going.

But alas, climaxes were not made to last. She sank into his chest to catch her breath, loving the way his arms came around her and held her tight. She loved him.

The realization hit her like a ton of bricks. She loved Carter Malone. Never before had she ever loved someone to the point where she couldn't imagine life without them. She swallowed, almost afraid to find out what he felt.

"Carter?" Ryan drew a heart on his pec.

"Hmm?" He'd settled farther down into the water, keeping them both warm.

"Were you serious...about the baby thing?"

"What baby thing?"

Shit. He didn't even remember. Damn men and what they

say in the heat of passion.

"Never mind."

His chest rumbled against her cheek but she couldn't bring herself to look at him. Her ears were hot with embarrassment.

"Do you mean the part about me wanting to see you round with my child?"

Ryan perked but said cautiously, "Uh-huh."

He tilted her face to his with a finger under her chin. "Most definitely." His lips touched hers tenderly. "At least three or four times."

She laughed. "Are you sure you're a man?"

He flexed his hips, making her groan. His cock was still hard inside her. Or getting hard again. "Pretty sure."

"So...what are you saying?" *Fish much, Ryan?*

"I think my biological clock is ticking. Meeting you changed something inside me. Then seeing my partner Ridge and his wife with their new baby made me jealous as all hell. I want that. With you. If you'll have me."

Ryan sat up. "Why, Carter Malone, are you proposing to me?"

"Yes." He grabbed her knuckles and kissed them. "Marry me. You have to."

"Why is that?"

"You mother said so."

"What?"

"Mmm-hmm. Her words were, 'You'll be good for my daughter.' Yesterday she told me to make sure I have you at her house for brunch on Sunday promptly at ten."

"Oh geez. The woman is relentless. If we don't show, there will be hell to pay."

Carter leaned over and licked a circle around her nipple. "We could tell her we were busy making her a grandchild."

"I haven't said yes."

"You will."

"What makes you so sure?" She gripped his head back so she could see into his eye

"Because I will never feel sorry for you

Ryan laughed out loud and ground h More water went over the edge to splash o

"So?" he asked, holding her in hi wiggle anymore.

"Yes. Yes, yes, yes. I love you." She'd

"I love you too, Ryan Cooper Dixon

She cradled his face in her hands deep. "Malone will suffice, thank you v pushing her over the edge. She held herself rigid against his chest. Apparently he'd primed her well because she'd come but he hadn't.

"Sorry, sweetheart." He gripped her hips to hold her down and drove upward. Her clit throbbed with each thrust, prolonging her orgasm. Again and again he filled her. Just as she thought she might miraculously come again, Carter stiffened beneath her. Even through the heat of the water she felt him pour into her, and for the first time wondered what it would be like if she weren't on the pill. He'd opened her eyes to the possibility. Was that really what he wanted?

He must have sensed that she was close because instead of basking in his own glory he pressed a thumb to her clit once more. The cylinders were all still firing, sending an arrow of tingling sensation straight to her womb.

"Come for me one more time, Ryan."

She tried, sought the release sitting so close she could taste it. The kicker that sent her over the edge was his mouth on her nipple, his teeth biting gently on the nub and wringing the orgasm from her. Ryan arched into it, urging the throbbing pulse at her clit to keep going.

But alas, climaxes were not made to last. She sank into his chest to catch her breath, loving the way his arms came around her and held her tight. She loved him.

The realization hit her like a ton of bricks. She loved Carter Malone. Never before had she ever loved someone to the point where she couldn't imagine life without them. She swallowed, almost afraid to find out what he felt.

"Carter?" Ryan drew a heart on his pec.

"Hmm?" He'd settled farther down into the water, keeping them both warm.

"Were you serious...about the baby thing?"

"What baby thing?"

Shit. He didn't even remember. Damn men and what they

say in the heat of passion.

"Never mind."

His chest rumbled against her cheek but she couldn't bring herself to look at him. Her ears were hot with embarrassment.

"Do you mean the part about me wanting to see you round with my child?"

Ryan perked but said cautiously, "Uh-huh."

He tilted her face to his with a finger under her chin. "Most definitely." His lips touched hers tenderly. "At least three or four times."

She laughed. "Are you sure you're a man?"

He flexed his hips, making her groan. His cock was still hard inside her. Or getting hard again. "Pretty sure."

"So...what are you saying?" *Fish much, Ryan?*

"I think my biological clock is ticking. Meeting you changed something inside me. Then seeing my partner Ridge and his wife with their new baby made me jealous as all hell. I want that. With you. If you'll have me."

Ryan sat up. "Why, Carter Malone, are you proposing to me?"

"Yes." He grabbed her knuckles and kissed them. "Marry me. You have to."

"Why is that?"

"You mother said so."

"What?"

"Mmm-hmm. Her words were, 'You'll be good for my daughter.' Yesterday she told me to make sure I have you at her house for brunch on Sunday promptly at ten."

"Oh geez. The woman is relentless. If we don't show, there will be hell to pay."

Carter leaned over and licked a circle around her nipple. "We could tell her we were busy making her a grandchild."

"I haven't said yes."

"You will."

"What makes you so sure?" She gripped his hair and pulled his head back so she could see into his eyes.

"Because I will never feel sorry for your sorry ass."

Ryan laughed out loud and ground herself on his erection. More water went over the edge to splash on the tile floor.

"So?" he asked, holding her in his lap so she couldn't wiggle anymore.

"Yes. Yes, yes, yes. I love you." She'd never been so happy.

"I love you too, Ryan Cooper Dixon Malone."

She cradled his face in her hands and kissed him, long and deep. "Malone will suffice, thank you very much."

To the Max

Dedication

To everyone who asked for Max. I loved writing him and Jordan and hope you enjoy reading about them. They're two of my favorite characters.

Chapter One

Max Jensen sang along with Nickelback's "Rockstar" as he followed the woman he was currently investigating. Annie Devlin's husband was positive his wife was having an affair. Normally Max would have passed the case on to one of his subordinates, but considering Jack had broken his ankle that morning and Kent was out sick, the job had landed in his lap.

He hated these cases. Hated chasing after women, or men, who couldn't keep their pants zipped, thus pissing off their respective spouses and causing *him* to have to waste time snooping when he could be working more exciting cases.

Which was exactly why, when his company had gotten big enough, he'd hired employees.

Mrs. Devlin exited the highway into a middle-class area. Max wondered what her husband would think if he discovered his wife was not only having an affair but slumming too. Mr. Devlin would for damn sure think anything less than his own worth to be slumming it. He would also likely divorce the woman rather than have to touch what he'd perceive as her dirtied hands.

At least, that was the impression Max had gotten from the man. He sort of understood why Mrs. Devlin would look elsewhere if she needed relief.

She drove a few miles more before turning into a dimly lit lot and parking. Max parallel parked his own vehicle across the street where he could still see her, then extracted his camera from the bag on the floor. He reached for the big daddy lens. No doubt he'd need to do some zooming in.

A small strip mall sat to the left of the lot, an apartment complex directly behind it and a convenience store to the right.

Twenty bucks she was headed for the apartments and her lover. Why else would she have come all this way, out of her comfort zone of diamonds, fine china and high tea?

The woman would make a great friend for his mother.

Max turned off the car and slouched back in the seat to wait Mrs. Devlin out. The street lamp cast an eerie glow on the white car in front of him, making it a disgusting shade of...newborn-shit, mustard yellow.

Worse though, was the fact he even knew the color of baby shit. He had Ridge Casey, one of his clients, to thank for that. The man's son was adorable, Max admitted, but stinky as hell. And if Ridge's partner, Carter Malone, and Ryan, Carter's wife, kept it up at the rate they seemed to go at it, another baby would be making its way into the Malone and Casey fold before the year was up.

Made Max shiver. A grown man shivering over the thought of having a baby.

He tucked the camera into his lap and unwrapped the PB&J he'd made on the fly. Eating with the whole color thing going on in front of him sorta made him want to regurgitate the bite he took. Then again, at the moment, Max was hungry enough to eat dirt. He could be out enjoying a steak if the client hadn't insisted he follow his wife.

"She always goes out all secretive on Friday nights," he'd said, pacing Max's office in his Armani suit. "And she's been...wanting sex." The man had seemed downright offended.

Max had almost snorted out loud but somehow held it in. Imagine someone's wife wanting sex. What was the world coming to? He'd wondered at the time why in the hell the pompous ass couldn't follow his own wife to her destination, but then the supremely rich felt those kinds of things were beneath them. They'd rather pay an exorbitant fee to have someone else do it.

Another thing that reminded him of his mother. She had a real knack for paying too much for any service available whether she needed it or not.

Several minutes passed before Mrs. Devlin got out of her car. Her head swiveled in every direction. She was definitely afraid someone would see her.

But see her doing what?

Finally she shut the door, wrapped her fists in the lapel of her ankle-length fur coat and walked briskly toward...the strip mall?

A giggling mass of girls exited one of the shops, followed by what Max guessed were their mothers, attracting his attention.

Max sat up in his seat and gripped the camera, ready to snap a few shots. "Where in the hell are you headed, Mrs. Devlin? Meeting a man at his work?"

He scanned the shops. A donut place, a dance studio from which the girls had exited, a UPS store, a Subway and a used bookstore.

Mrs. Devlin paused on the walk to let the girls pass. The way she stuck herself against the brick wall, she almost looked like she thought the girls would sully her somehow. She shielded her face by turning into the wall and covering the other side with her hand.

What in the shit? Did she think a bunch of eight-year-olds would recognize her?

When the group had passed, Mrs. Devlin again looked around. As soon as she was sure the coast was clear she continued on.

And stopped at the dance studio.

So she was meeting a young, nimble dance stud then. Interesting.

She glanced to her right and left, tugged the door open and

quickly disappeared inside.

Movement behind the window had him lifting his binoculars instead of the camera. A tall, lithe woman paced, sort of bouncing on the balls of her feet as she twisted long coffee-colored hair into a knot on top of her head. With the direction she faced he couldn't see her exact features, but what he could view was the rise of her breasts as she reached upward.

Damn they'd be a small handful. Just the right amount. Gorgeous. Outlined succulently by a thin black leotard which he suddenly felt the need to peel off her to reveal her skin inch by inch until he'd divested her body of the skimpy piece of clothing.

She had to be commando beneath it because from the view he had with the lens that could pick up a playing card at five hundred yards, there were no panty lines in the skintight material.

"Damn it." The woman glided away before he could look his fill. Not that there was enough time in the day to do so. He figured he'd need several weeks for that.

With a groan he slumped into the seat. "On a fucking job and fantasizing about the scenery. Nice, Maxo. Real professional."

A few minutes later three women jaunted up the sidewalk, headed for the same place. The way they laughed and clung to each other made Max think perhaps they'd imbibed something before making their way to the studio.

Would make for an interesting ballet session.

There were a few more stragglers, ladies who waltzed into the studio just after six. Then the blinds used to shield the window during the day were tilted upward. Not closed, because light still spilled out.

"Damn it." He wouldn't be able to see inside from his position. He'd have to be up above the window to see down in, or standing at the window itself. Too bad he didn't have x-ray lenses.

Max waited a good ten minutes to make sure no one else showed up, then grabbed his coat from the passenger seat and climbed out of the nondescript Chevy Impala. Missing the luxury of his Lexus, he stretched his six-foot-three frame to wring out most of the kinks he'd acquired from sitting in the cramped space. Whistling, he crossed the street, hands in the pockets of his leather jacket, and peered between the slats. Thank God it was winter and the streets were lonely after dark or he'd look like some sort of Peeping Tom.

What he saw would make any male above the age of twelve choke on his own spit. His breath fogged the glass in the cold night air, and he fought the temptation to reach for his suddenly throbbing cock.

Two things registered at once.

One, this was no fucking ballet class. The beautiful woman he'd seen in the window had her sweet, tight, firm, lithe body wrapped around a silver pole, undulating with the pulse of music he could barely hear, her head dropped back in ecstasy.

And two, this job was officially over because Mrs. Devlin wasn't having an affair. Her secretive Friday night rendezvous were with a pole.

Jordan spread her legs in a wide V, almost in a splits position, and pressed her nose to the floor. Sweat dripped from her forehead to plop on the mat beneath her, and she welcomed it. She'd worked her class harder than ever before simply because she'd been pissed and needed to burn off the energy.

Dirk Clement, the asshole, had come on to her again that morning, and she'd had to practically fight her way out of his clutches. The bastard was lucky he wasn't sporting a black eye or squished balls right now.

Loosening the tightness of her spine, she sank farther down and sighed. "I have to quit my job."

"What was that, Jordan?"

Jordan looked up and planted her chin on her crossed forearms. "Nothing. Talking to myself." She'd forgotten her students were still around, stretching themselves in the hope they wouldn't be sore in the morning.

"You know, if I could get into that position, I wouldn't need to come to your class to impress Mike." Clare's eyes gleamed with her grin.

Her friend, Mia, snorted. "Honey, I got news for you. It would take a hell of a lot less than folding your body in half to impress Mike. Bending over and wiggling your ass would suffice."

"Then why the hell are we here shaking our thing around this pole?"

"Because if you want anything other than *wham bam thank you, ma'am* out of a man, you've got to work it. Make him wait for it."

"Right," added Christy, the third friend of the trio, "because pole dancing in front of him won't make him so damn horny that the second he gets his dick in you he'll explode and be done for the night, leaving you unsatisfied yet again. I think we're doing it backwards, girls."

"I don't know." Four heads turned to the corner where Annie was thoroughly bundling herself back into her coat. "It seems to be working for my husband."

Since Annie rarely spoke and was by far the most repressed woman in the class, Jordan was astonished by the soft admission. Annie seemed to realize she'd spoken the words out loud because her cheeks burned bright red and she visibly swallowed before shoving her feet in her boots and running for the door. Sprinting might have been a more apt word.

The friends burst out laughing as soon as the door slammed shut. Jordan sat up, smiling also, and tucked her legs into a butterfly position to continue stretching. She hadn't been kidding about working her ass off. Even she might be sore in the morning. But hey, she'd gotten over her anger.

Somewhat.

Enough to hopefully sleep through the night without feeling Dirk's groping hands touching her body.

"God, who'd've thunk it? Annie gettin' it on with the kink." Christy twisted at the waist and leaned to the side, her long arm extended over her head.

Mia laughed again—who wouldn't with the image of staid Annie in kink mode? "The woman hasn't spoken more than ten words in five months and she drops that little bomb?"

"It's always the quiet ones," Christy offered. "Shy girls always get the best sex, don't they?"

"Then you must be getting none, huh?" Jordan couldn't resist the taunt. Christy was the most vocal of the class, often making the eight students crack up with the latest bits of her life.

Not that Jordan could talk. When was the last time she'd done the horizontal mambo? A year ago? Two? So long ago her out-of-date contraceptive devices would more likely *help* her conceive rather than protect her.

"Hardy har." Christy jerked her head in quick succession to both sides, popping her neck. "I'll have you know I'm meeting a man tonight at the bar."

"Meeting one or seducing one?" Mia laid back on the mat, her arms and legs akimbo.

"Hopefully both," Christy said truthfully.

Jordan suddenly felt jealous. She wanted to *meet* a man. Wanted to seduce some stranger and have a night of unrequited lovemaking. One with no regrets in the morning and no awkward goodbyes. Hell she'd settle for pretty much anything at this point. Anything as long as she got to feel a cock between her thighs, buried deep inside her while her lover sucked and tugged at her nipples.

Jesus, she had it bad. She jumped to her feet, determined

not to let the girls and their naughty thoughts drive her into a frenzy.

She should do it though. Head to the bar and pick up some man. Relive her college years, the glory days of her youth, when nothing and no one was going to stop her from doing anything.

Ten years could certainly change a woman, couldn't they? Now where was she? Cleaning houses for the rich, some of whom felt too entitled to clean up at all after themselves, and teaching ballet/pole-dancing aerobics instead of owning her own studio. At the rate she was going, her studio dreams were about fifty years out of reach.

Perhaps not quite that far, but still. Securing a loan for a place in a decent neighborhood for a woman with no means of financial backup wasn't easy. And with the present economy, the outlook was even less pretty. No bank wanted to fund her. Sure, she could throw her family's name around and have any amount at her disposal in the snap of her fingers, but that would mean using her background to get what she wanted.

No way in hell would she ever accept help from her parents.

Not that they'd give it. They hadn't forgiven her for choosing the path in life she had. Snobs. Christ, they'd even tried to tell her once who she should marry.

Enough. She wasn't going to go there. Not after the day she'd had and how hard she'd worked to shove it out of her system. Adding her family to the mix would only piss her off more.

Jordan bit her lip and made a decision. No more whining and moaning. Tonight she was going to do something about her misery. At least one of her miseries anyway.

Tonight she was going to get laid.

"Hey," she said, surprising the girls as they pulled their weary bodies to the benches that held their things. "Would you mind if I tagged along to this meet and seduce?"

Three mouths dropped open, but Jordan wasn't about to be

deterred. She hopped to her feet, bouncing with an excitement she hadn't felt in a while.

"No."

"Sweet."

"Of course you can."

They answered together.

"Great. Where should I meet you?" Her mind was already doing a mental search of her closet and what to wear.

"We're going to Down Under. It's *ladies'* night." Mia smacked her lips.

"Perfect." Jordan grinned and started gathering her things. "What time?"

"Nine thirty. For some reason I never pictured you trolling for men, Jordan." Mia eyed her up and down as if seeing someone new instead of the dance instructor they were familiar with.

Jordan felt sort of new. Giddy. Needy.

She was going to get some.

She laughed. "I just decided I needed a distraction. What better way to distract myself than with the lesser species?"

"Amen to that sister." Clare put her hand up for a high five.

"Can't imagine why we thought you were any different than us," Christy purred. "You do teach pole dancing after all."

"Helps pay the bills." Jordan yanked her jeans over her leotard and buttoned them. "Not to mention what it does for your abs."

"Trust me, we know." Mia groaned and covered her stomach. "And what the shit was up with the sadistic workout tonight?"

Jordan shrugged. "I had some energy to release."

"I've got a far better way to work off excess energy than this." Christy gestured to the poles Dance Inc. had installed specifically in the back of the room for the growing-inpopularity class.

Jordan sure hoped the hell so. She wondered how rusty she really was at picking up guys.

"I hope I haven't lost it. It's been a while." Was she doing the right thing?

"Oh, honey," cooed Mia, "you shake your booty on the dance floor the way you do on those poles and you won't have any trouble gettin' some."

Everyone laughed again.

Jordan stamped her feet into her boots and laced them up before pulling her coat on and grabbing her helmet from its cubby. There was still another class, a late adult tap class, and since that teacher was there waiting for it, Jordan didn't need to lock up or anything. They walked out together.

"So we'll see you in a bit?" Christy eyed her dubiously as if she thought Jordan would change her mind.

"Absolutely. I'll be there." *With bells on.* She wouldn't miss this opportunity even if a loan agent fell from the sky with a contract in his hand.

Okay, yeah she would. But since such a scenario wasn't likely to happen...

The girls went one way after waving their goodbyes and Jordan went the other, headed for her prized possession. Stuffing her sweaty head into the full-shield helmet, she swung her leg over the cobalt blue Yamaha FZ6, her pride and joy, inserted the key and pushed the ignition button with her right thumb. She loved the sound of the bike as it revved to life. Tonight, for once, she was going to get more action than the vibration of her bike between her legs.

Chapter Two

Max groaned and dropped onto a stool at the bar of Down Under. His blood pressure had nearly blasted through the atmosphere on the way here. Watching the kamikaze on that projectile some people commonly referred to as a motorcycle had left Max with heart palpitations and fingers that would no longer straighten. He hadn't even realized he'd been squeezing the steering wheel to death until she'd come to a complete stop and hopped off the death trap to disappear rather quickly into an apartment building.

Why he'd stuck around and followed her to her home he didn't know. Something about the woman had made him sit in his uncomfortable car and wait for her though. Even when Annie Devlin had gone, taking her nonexistent case with her, he'd been too captivated to leave. Thank God, because then he'd seen the woman get on the motorcycle. He'd only just gotten his heart rate and breathing close to normal when she'd skipped out of her place again, dressed in a different pair of slim, butt-hugging jeans, and gotten back on the damn blue bullet. She'd swept her almost-black hair into a low ponytail and stuck her head into the helmet once more, and it had been all Max could do not to dart across the street and yank her off the beast if for no other reason than to keep himself from having a coronary.

She'd been grinning like a loon. He wondered what her mother thought of her little girl on a bike.

Perhaps her mother didn't have a clue. There wasn't much

his own mother knew about what he did.

Max should have left right then instead of stalking her like some kind of deranged lunatic. He should have gone home, done the paperwork to close the Devlin case and washed his hands of the suicidal woman. But no. For some indefinable reason he couldn't imagine letting her take off on that damn piece of machinery without following her to make sure she arrived alive to wherever she was headed in such a blissful mood.

Sixty-seven fucking miles per hour on the goddamn highway and fifteen minutes later, here he sat, ready to drink away the pounding in his chest and the renewed ache in his permanently curled fingers.

And make sure she didn't drink too much then get on her damned little crotch rocket again.

All the times he'd seen a motorcycle on the road and never thought a thing of it, and one little woman had brought out every protective instinct in his body.

You don't even know her name, Jensen.

His dick didn't care. All it knew was that the woman was fucking hot.

The live band's music drummed into his head, amplifying the headache brought about by her stunt driving. From where he sat he could see her and the women from her class whom she'd met outside. They were seated at a round table to his nine o'clock, all of them laughing and throwing their heads back at something the redhead said.

Kamikaze's long throat drew his attention. He wanted to swipe his tongue up and down the column, tasting her. He wanted to take in the scent of her right there behind the lobe of the ear graced with a high-cartilage piercing. He wanted to know if she had any other piercings. Like her navel or her pussy. Did his pole dancer have her clit pierced?

Jesus Christ, Jensen. She's not your fucking anything. What would his mother say if he brought home a pole dancer for

152

Sunday dinner? Not that he gave a rat's ass what she said. Well, actually, it might be freaking hilarious to see his mother's face when kamikaze disclosed her occupation. He slapped his hand on the bar. "Shit. She's got you tied in knots, doesn't she?"

"What's that, mate?"

Max jumped at the bartender's Australian accent and cleared his throat. "Nothing. I'll have a Fosters." She'd fucking driven him to drink on duty.

But then, he wasn't technically on duty anymore. Mrs. Devlin hadn't been having an affair tonight, and he'd seen her on her way, not sweaty from sex but instead a thorough swing on a pole. He'd done his job, so this was after hours. Time to relax, throw back a beer or two and watch the—he glanced up at the muted TV in the corner—rugby match?

"Here ya go, mate. Fosters. Long day?"

It took a moment for Max to understand what *long die* meant. "No. Just a long-ass afternoon." *And an even longer night tailing a kamikaze with a death wish.*

Okay, so she hadn't been crazy on her bike. Hadn't done any of the stupid shit he'd seen some punks doing for fun when it was really dangerous as hell. Like standing on the seat doing eighty on the highway or popping a wheelie in the middle of traffic. Yeah, she'd sped a tiny bit, but no more than the rest of the traffic. She'd actually handled the thing pretty damn well now that he looked back on it.

"Find yourself a nice partner and take a load off, mate. Tomorrow will look better."

If he woke up next to a certain partner it might.

Damn. He had to stop thinking of her in terms of sex. He didn't even know her name, had only discovered her because of a job. How likely was it she would wind up in his bed? No matter how goddamn beautiful she was or how fucking hard she made his dick, he had to remember he didn't know anything about her. Other than the fact she could wrap herself oh so sweetly around a shiny silver pole.

Get control of yourself, Maximillian. That's what his mother would say. And he knew what would come next. *Unscrew your penis and put it on the shelf. Jensen men do not think with their little heads, no matter what your father does.* She always said *penis* too. Nothing vulgar would ever come out of Kara Patterson-Jensen's mouth, but she sure as hell would never mince words either. God help you if you ever spoke back to her.

As the black sheep of the family, Max mostly got the cold shoulder, chin raise, sniffle and glare. His mother chose to ignore the career Max had craved since he was nine years old when the security company paid to keep him safe had done their job. If his bodyguard at the time, and later Max's mentor, Richard, hadn't laid his life on the line, Max would be twenty-some years in the grave.

Richard had taken a bullet to protect his young charge, and Max, even at nine, had vowed to repay the older man in any way possible. After years of showing him the ropes, Richard had helped Max form his own company specializing in security and PI-type work. Another thing Max felt needed repayment.

He wondered what Richard would think of Max's distraction. He had, after all, pretty much dismissed the case the second he'd seen Mrs. Devlin in her, um, *dance* class. Just because he hadn't seen the woman with a man tonight didn't mean she wasn't having an affair.

Who the hell was he kidding? The woman was hiding her affinity for pole dancing. That's all.

Max lifted the bottle to his lips and took a drag. His gaze wandered back to the table where *she* sat, and he nearly choked. All four women were eyeing him like he was a prime piece of meat to be devoured.

"There ya go, mate." The bartender nudged Max's shoulder. "Night's lookin' better already."

A tiny smile tilted the kamikaze's lips before she turned away, and damned if the come-get-me look didn't make his zipper dig into his erection.

He borrowed a widely known mantra and changed it to suit his situation.

I will not have sexual relations with that woman. I will not have sexual relations with that woman.

It would be wrong, right?

She stood, her round, perfectly palm-sized breasts pressing against the fabric of the silky shirt she wore, her ass cupped in that pair of skinny jeans he wanted to peel away inch by inch. She'd taken the elastic from her hair so the gorgeous strands swung freely around her shoulders and attempted to hide the nipples he swore he could see poking through the thin material covering them, despite the dim light.

Then she took a step toward him, and another, this time more hesitant. Her head turned in the direction of her friends, and she shushed them with a finger at her lips.

Sure he was drooling, Max swallowed and gulped down the remainder of his beer. If he didn't leave before Kamikaze got to him, he'd have her stripped naked and thrown belly down on the bar, his cock thrust inside her sheath before she could say hello.

She flicked another glance his direction then fled to a hallway under a sign that read Restrooms.

Well, if that didn't beat all. Max leaned both elbows on the table and ordered another beer.

What on earth was she doing trying to pick up a stranger at a bar?

Sex, Jordan. Remember the sex you wanted to have to rehydrate your parched woman's parts? The ones currently shriveling up from lack of action?

With ultimate resolve, she lifted her face and stared at herself in the mirror.

"Jordan, you will go out there and seduce that walking sex

God."

A snicker behind her made her jump.

"You go, girl. Hey, while you're handing out the confidence, mind sharing some with me? There's this really hot guy out there I'd do just about anything to go to bed with."

Jordan smiled and told herself not to punch the woman. Surely she wasn't referring to the same guy. There were lots of other men in the bar.

But only one who'd been built specifically for causing a woman to orgasm with a simple touch. Jordan was sure that would be the outcome if she ever got the nerves to get close enough to him.

Enough. She was here for sex, she was going to get some. Self-doubt was not going to dissuade her.

"Sure," she said to the woman washing her hands. "As long as we're not after the same one. I'm not into threesomes." *And I really don't want to go to jail for breaking your neck. Tall, dark and drool-worthy is mine, mine and all mine.*

The woman's laugh grated on Jordan's nerves, tempting her to strangle the bleached blonde's neck just to get her to tell her who she was lusting after.

"Oh, my God, he's like, so cute. Red hair..."

Jordan didn't hear another word over the breath she let out. Time to buck up and become a woman all over again. If luck was on her side tonight, the stud at the bar was going home with her.

Or she was going home with him.

She'd lived the last few years in anonymity, surely she could pick up one man and not be found out. He hadn't seemed to recognize her at least.

Jesus, she was doing it again. The urge to slap herself grew. Where was the set of *cojones* she'd used to move out of her parents' and live her own life away from all the crap money entailed? She straightened, flipped her hair over her shoulder and checked to make sure she didn't have anything green between her teeth. That'd be a mood killer for sure.

She was here to get her sex on.

"Good luck." Jordan shoved through the door and headed straight for the bar. If he wasn't still sitting there, she would cry.

"Go get him, Jordan," she heard from the friends she'd come with. It gave her courage. Hell yes she'd get him. She'd use his body as her pole and show him all kinds of new moves.

His closely shaved dark brown head hung over his beer and his shoulders were slumped. Damn. She'd thought he'd been interested. She hadn't mistaken the way his nostrils had flared when she'd started toward him earlier or the way his eyes had widened. There'd been a flash of lust, damn it. On both their parts.

Jordan was suddenly close enough to reach out and touch him. Mmm...he smelled so good. Like man and cologne and yum all rolled into one, and she smelled it even over all the combined alcohol and smoke odors of the bar.

It was do-or-die time. Jordan tapped him on the back. "Hello."

His head whipped back so fast she was amazed he didn't give himself whiplash or fly off the stool. Catching himself before that happened, he darted a glance between her and her friends before settling on her face.

His eyes were green. Pale green. Beautiful. Her panties went wet just looking into his gaze.

At least she knew she hadn't dried up quite yet.

"Hello." Oh man, the sound of his voice made her shiver. Deep and sensual. It curled around her to the point she swore she could feel his mouth moving on her throat.

"I'm Jordan." Did she stick out a hand to shake? Where the hell was her inner college chick?

"Max."

Max. Perfect. She wanted Max. Right here, right now. If only clicking her heels together and pronouncing, "There's no place like home, there's no place like home," would get her anywhere.

He seemed to contemplate something. It made her nervous. Picking up men used to be so easy. Of course those were the days of trying to attract the media attention just to piss her mother off. Right now, Max was going to give her a complex.

"You wanna dance, Jordan?" He said her name like he was trying it out on his tongue.

She wanted to shout, "Try my clit out with your tongue too, please."

She refrained. No use scaring the man off before she'd gotten out of tonight what she wanted.

He hopped off the barstool—or stood at any rate—and towered over her five-foot-six frame. Maximillian. Maximillian? Is that how she saw him? Appropriate because right this second she felt like she'd just won a million bucks. He had to be a good few inches beyond six feet, muscular too, as evidenced by the fit of his shirt beneath his leather jacket. She wanted to rip the shirt off and lick his abs, see if he tasted as good as he smelled.

Please God let him be this big across the board. She needed big. Needed to be filled to capacity plus some. Her clit actually ached at the thought of him between her legs.

She'd turned into a hooker. A pole-dancing, stranger-picking-up, begging-for-big hooker.

The devil on her shoulder was going to win hands down over the angel telling her to go slow.

"I'd love to dance." *Horizontally on a mattress.* Could one portray one's need with just a look? Can you say skank? She ought to be ashamed of herself.

He took her hand in his and led her to the jumble of bodies shaking it to the music on the wooden floor. There was a clap and cheer behind her, and Jordan almost flipped off the three girls she'd come with.

"Your friends are happy for you?"

Lord she loved his voice and how it practically vibrated across her skin. "I guess." As if she was going to tell him, *Of course they are. We came here trolling for men and I've already landed one. You. Congratulations. You won an out-of-practice, dried-up pole dancer. Woohoo!*

Yeah, that'd go over real well.

"You don't do this much, do you?"

Fuu-udge. He could friggin' tell that? "No. Not really. Well, not in a while anyway." He didn't need to know just how long it had actually been.

His right palm held her left hand with gentle ease, and his other hand came around her waist to rest at the small of her back, his long fingers practically spanning her waistline. She wondered if he'd slip it lower, cop a feel.

Please God, cop a feel. There was the inner college vixen. Course, back then she'd have reached behind there and moved it for him if he hadn't done it fast enough.

Which Max didn't.

She bit her lip. A pole-dancing aerobics instructor and she was stiff as a board. What happened to making him the pole?

He pulled her to him with a quick jerk, and she suddenly found her belly pressed against a rather solid object. A long, hard, thick object by the feel of it. She looked up into his face and read the desire written on every millimeter. Day-old scruff on his cheeks made him seem even more rugged. Her legs wobbled with the thought of those tiny whiskers scraping on the inside of her thighs and the sensitive skin of her pussy.

"I'd be lying if I said I didn't want to be with you tonight." His breath fanned over her lips, he was so close.

"Me too."

"Good."

She kissed him. Stretched the two or three inches that

separated them as he leaned down, and kissed him, opening her mouth to his and pushing her tongue inside. He tasted like the beer he'd been drinking, but she didn't give a damn. She only cared that the man she'd seen across the room and lusted over immediately wanted her as much as she wanted him.

She was going to sleep with a stranger.

No, she was going to make love to a stranger. Jordan had a strong suspicion that when they finally reached a bed there would be no sleeping involved.

Now why did the mere idea give her such a thrill?

Chapter Three

Max tilted his head and took over the kiss, all the while calling himself ten kinds of fool. She was sweet, and more potent than any alcohol. He was definitely leaving this bar drunk on something tonight, but he most certainly wouldn't be leaving alone.

"I shouldn't be doing this," he murmured at her ear before kissing a path down her jaw line and back to the sensuous mouth waiting for him. He wanted to see her lips tight around his cock, wanted to see those baby blues looking up at him from her kneeling position on the floor.

"Me neither." Her fingernails dug into his shoulders and one of her feet lifted to climb his leg as she tried to fit her pussy against his cock. With his height it wasn't happening for her, and he sensed her frustration.

He was going to have to fire himself for fraternizing with a...what? She wasn't anything to him, he reminded himself. He'd met her while on the job.

Sort of.

Stalked her more like. And that made him a criminal.

He should be trailing his own ass and taking pictures.

A soft moan escaped Jordan's lips, wringing Max out of his thoughts.

"Is this what you want, kamikaze?" He slipped his hand between them and cupped her mound.

She groaned with relief and ground herself on the heel of his hand, her perfect white teeth coming out to bite at her lower lip.

"Kamikaze?" Jordan gasped when he rubbed her harder through the denim she wore.

"Yeah." He nibbled on her ear and hoped like hell his hand was somewhat hidden from view as they were still standing on the dance floor. A glance up showed no one was paying attention anyway.

If she thought anything about the nickname he'd given her, she'd already forgotten it. Her eyes were glazing over. She was close, he could tell by the way she held her body stiff.

But what he really wanted to see was just how limber she could be.

Max yanked his hand from between them but kept her tight to him. He spoke against her temple and rocked her down from her near climax.

"My place or yours?" Whichever was fucking closest he hoped. He was about to come without her even touching his most critical parts.

"Which is closest?"

He smiled. "I'm in Clayton."

She angled her head back and looked appalled. "That's too far."

"So we go to your place. Unless you're not comfortable with that. We can always go the hotel route."

"I'm not far from here."

He knew that, of course, having just followed her home from the studio and then to the bar, but tipping his hat to that knowledge would have her fleeing like a doe in the crosshairs. And rightfully so.

"You sure?" No matter what, he wasn't into forcing a woman. He wanted her to feel safe.

"Positive. Let's go." She started tugging him across the

floor, and he laughed. Minx.

Part of him wondered if his little pole-dancing kamikaze did this often—which pissed him off. The other part wondered, based on certain reactions he'd witnessed earlier from her, if she did this at all. She'd said she hadn't done this in a while but what did that mean? A day, a month? A year?

A pole-dancing virgin? No way. He knew instinctively she was no virgin.

Damn. He suddenly hoped she had a practice pole at home. His dick hardened to the point of pain behind his fly at the image of a private dance, her in nothing but her panties...and then in nothing at all.

Jordan stopped at the table he'd seen her at before. A man now graced the seat she'd had.

"Hey, Jordan. This is Mike," one of the girls said.

Jordan and her energy practically bounced. She tugged her coat off the back of Mike's chair and jerked it on. It only served to remind Max he'd never taken his off.

"Nice to meet you. I'm leaving now."

"But we just got here." This from another of the women who knew exactly where Jordan was headed, based on the gleam in her eye.

"You stay then. I... We're... This is Maximillian." She sucked in a breath and Max narrowed his eyes. How the fuck had she known his name? "Max." She turned to him. "Sorry about the Maximillian. It suited you. I really have no idea if that's your real name."

It suited him like a giant pimple on his ass. Maximillian was the name his mother had given him. His snob name. Then again when Jordan said it... "No problem."

"Okay." She turned back to her friends. "So. See you next week?"

"Uh-huh." The third woman spoke this time, she too smiling with secret knowledge.

Jordan bent to retrieve something from beneath the table, giving Max a beautiful view of her perfect jeans-covered ass and a nice slice of skin where her shirt rode up. He had to bite the inside of his cheek to keep from grabbing her hips and thrusting against her.

Time for that later. When there were no clothes to separate them.

When she straightened she held her helmet in her hand, and his erection ran off like a scared rabbit. Jesus Christ, he'd forgotten she had to ride that damn thing again. With all the coiled energy she was currently harboring, that bullet of hers was going to prove to be too much to handle.

He'd be wiping her body off the pavement instead of lifting her in his arms to bathe her after fucking her senseless. He fisted his hands. Max had been on the wrong end of a Glock protecting a governor, gotten stabbed twice, shot at when he was nine and attacked by a dog at thirteen but nothing, *nothing* scared him more than seeing his kamikaze on that bike.

"Alrighty then. Max?"

"Yep. Let's go." He put his hand just above her cute butt and escorted her to the door, dreading what was about to occur but powerless to do anything lest he give himself away. A chorus of goodbyes serenaded them out.

She walked quickly, matching her strides with his, obviously just as anxious to be with him as he was to be with her. Now he'd do anything to be heading back to his place in his car.

"You ride?" What the hell else was he going to say?

"Oh. Yeah. I'm not fast or anything so I think you'll be able to keep up." She winked at him. Actually fucking winked.

He wondered what she'd think of him if he admitted to her that watching her ride the fucking motorcycle made him a sweaty, nauseous mess.

Resting the helmet on the seat, Jordan pulled her hair into

the ponytail as she'd done earlier. "Where are you parked?"

He nodded in the direction of the Chevy. Now more than ever he wished for his Lexus. What kind of man would she see him as to be driving what amounted to be an unmarked police car?

His fucking mother was showing through. Only a snob would think in terms of a woman seeing who he was by the car he drove.

Jordan yanked on the helmet and strapped it below her chin. He was tempted to knock on it to make sure it was real then try and tug it off to see if it was good and secure on her sweet noggin.

If he didn't fucking get the image of her wrapped in road rash out of his head, he'd never be able to give them what they both wanted because his dick would remain permanently wilted.

Weren't guys supposed to be turned on by chicks on bikes?

"I'm actually only about fifteen minutes from here."

"Okay." Should be more like twenty, but okay. He was turning into a fucking pussy. "Do you have a car?" he couldn't resist asking.

"Yeah. For my job. Have to carry stuff. But I *love* my bike. Wouldn't trade it for the world."

He'd have to think of something to entice her away from it then.

Shit. What the hell, Jensen? She's a fling when you should have unscrewed your dick and put it on the shelf, remember? Neither of them was looking for forever here.

He ripped his keys from his pocket in a vicious movement.

"Hey," she said, putting her hand on his cheek and looking at him from behind the open visor. Damn helmet made her head look big, he groused silently.

"You okay with this?"

He wanted to yell "no" and throw her over his shoulder and

stuff her into the backseat of his car. "I have a feeling you're going to make me nervous on this thing."

She laughed. "It's not me I worry about, it's everyone else."

Exactly, goddamn it.

Her face went soft. "I want to kiss you."

His dick went hard. "Kinda difficult with that thing on your head."

"But you can take it off me when we get home. It and more," she promised.

"Christ."

She leaned as close as she could get with the helmet in the way and whispered near his ear. "I think I can make up for your nervousness of having to watch me ride."

Max grabbed her helmet with both hands and rested his forehead on it so he could still see her. "I'm going to hold you to that."

The vibration of the bike on her clit had not made her life any easier. It had been all she could do not to pull over and tell him to fuck trying to make it to her apartment. Was it possible to orgasm by motorcycle alone?

Jordan slipped off the seat after pulling into her spot next to her more sensible red Honda hatchback, a car she'd picked up used for a good price to haul all her cleaning supplies from job to job. Her mother would have a coronary if she ever saw Jordan's modes of transportation. She smiled and patted the seat before yanking off the helmet and shaking her head.

If ever there was a time not to think about one's mother, now was it.

Max's headlights blinded her for a moment as he turned into an empty space three spots beyond hers. He drove the kind of car that perfectly blended in. Sort of like her hatchback. It reminded her of an unmarked police car. Could he be...? Nah. She hadn't noticed a gun anywhere on his person, not that he couldn't have taken it off. He had been at a bar after all, but he would have told her if he was a policeman.

Right?

Didn't matter. He could be a chimney sweep for all she cared. She cleaned houses for a current living, wasn't like she could talk about career choices.

Her heart stuttered when the top of his dark crew-cut head emerged. How the hell did he fit in there without causing himself some serious muscle pain?

Jordan licked her lips as he drew closer to her. Stalked was a more apt word. She felt like a lamb in front of the lion. What was that phrase she'd heard? Stupid lamb.

The corners of his lips turned up. His hand came up to cup her left cheek. She sucked in a breath and shivered at the touch. His lips descended onto hers and his tongue swept into her mouth.

Oh Jesus, was she ever the stupid, stupid lamb. Max would devour her whole and leave her a blubbering puddle of goo.

But by God she was going to enjoy every second of her consumption.

He tasted like mint now. Preparing for them to be together? So sweet. Jordan wrapped her arms around his neck and angled her head for better access. He deepened the kiss, taking what she offered willingly. Her clit tingled in response, her nipples hardened.

Her human pole was oh so enticing. She had to move this show inside.

Not to mention it was damn cold outside.

"I'm on the first floor," she whispered against his mouth and gasped when his hand lowered to the small of her back and hugged her body to his. His erection pressed into her belly, telling her he was still just as interested as she.

He put his forehead on hers. "I don't like that bike, kamikaze. Scares me."

"I'm sorry."

"Are you?"

"Not so much."

He smiled and tugged her head back with a fist in her hair. "I think you'll have to make me hard again."

Jordan hitched her leg up and put her knee over his hip, rubbing her pussy on his erection. "You don't seem to be having trouble in that department."

"Minx."

"I think that's one step up from kamikaze."

He brought both hands around her and squeezed her buttocks. "You promised I could divest you of some clothes when we got here." The soft growl at her ear sent a wave of goose bumps over her skin.

"So let's go."

Max turned her and with his hands on her shoulders followed her to the front door of her apartment. For a split second as she stuck the key in the lock, she wondered if she was completely insane for inviting someone she knew nothing about into her home.

Chapter Four

Max took a deep breath and shook off his wayward doubts. He was doing nothing wrong. Consensual sex with a beautiful woman who wasn't in any way associated with a client.

Shit. He'd drive himself crazy with this line of thought. She'd come to *him* at Down Under, not the other way around.

Right, because following the woman wasn't weird.

Jordan threw the door to her apartment open and stepped inside. Max hesitated until she turned and beckoned him with a crook of her finger and a come-get-me smile.

He was a man above all else and there wasn't a man on the face of the earth who could resist the temptation before him. He shrugged out of his leather jacket and dropped it inside the foyer before kicking the door shut behind him with his heel. His intention had been to grasp Jordan's face in his hands and seize her lips but she had other ideas.

She leapt on him, pushing him back on the door. He caught her under her ass, holding her squirming form as she attacked his mouth like a starving animal. So much for running the show.

Panting, Jordan jerked back and stared at him. "Wait."

Wait? She wanted him to wait?

"I just want you to know I don't do this often. Never. I never do this. Well not since college anyway and even then I didn't do it a lot—"

Max held her in one arm and put a finger over her mouth. "Shh."

Chest still heaving, she closed her eyes. "I'm sorry."

"Nothing to be sorry about. You say no, we stop. Easy as that." *Please God, don't say no.*

"I won't say no." She wiggled out of his hold, her eyes glittering with a heat that made him hard as granite.

She slipped to her knees, her gaze never leaving his, her fingernails trailing down his abdomen to stop at the button fly of his jeans where she deftly unbuttoned him.

"Fuck." Max fisted his hands as her fingers slipped into the waist of his jeans and boxers and slowly pushed them to his knees. His T-shirt got hung up for a second on his dick where it jutted out. He forced himself not to take her head in his hands and thrust into her mouth. He had to let her set the pace.

"Mmm."

Mmm? What the hell did "mmm" mean? *Mmm, yum, I want to lick you dry,* or *Mmm, I'm not sure I can do this?*

Jordan surveyed him from every angle, and despite the fact that Max stood six foot two, weighed two hundred pounds and could take down an opponent in about twenty different ways, he suddenly found himself self-conscious. If he were a virgin, he might find his erection wilting under the scrutiny.

"Sorry. Just deciding where to start."

Shit. Max closed his eyes and swallowed. "You don't have to do this, Jordan."

"Oh, yes, I do." Without touching him she leaned in and pressed her tongue to the base of his penis.

The saliva got caught in his throat, choking him.

She licked him from root to tip, pausing to flick across the sensitive bundle of nerves of the frenulum, which made his eyes cross, before settling at the weeping hole and sucking the head into the hot recesses of her mouth.

"Oh. Shit."

He'd had blow jobs before. Many of them. In the past. So why was this one so different?

She sank down farther on him, attempting to take all of him. He didn't want her to choke and brought his hand up to her hair to pull her back.

She slapped his hand away.

"Damn it, Jordan."

"Mmm."

Oh, motherfucker, Jesus Christ. The hum sizzled along his dick to the base of his spine. His head hit the door with a thunk just as the head of his cock hit the back of her throat. When he glanced down she'd taken his entire length. Holy. Shit.

Jordan backed off, her tongue doing some wicked swirl along the way, and her cheeks hollowing with the force of her suction. She released him with a pop. One of her hands cupped his balls and the other wrapped around his cock. She pulled downward on his sac while twisting her spit-slicked fingers around the base, creating a dual sens—ah, make that tri sensation. Her lips surrounded the head again.

"Jordan..." he cautioned. He was seriously close to coming in a seriously short amount of time.

"Mmm."

Oh, payback was going to be sweet. He slammed his head against the door once more and gripped the wood trim with his fingertips.

Sweat beaded on his forehead. His knees wobbled like a virgin's. He shifted his stance, widening his feet as far as his jeans-hampered legs would allow him for better balance.

And then she touched him, a fingertip pressure behind his balls, pushing on his perineum, making him gasp.

"Shit." He couldn't remember ever being reduced to one-word phrases while getting sucked off.

The finger moved farther back to the tight ring of his anus. Max's eyes rolled back. There was nothing he could do to hold

171

out, not with a finger on his ass, a tug on his balls, a twist on his dick and a vacuum on his cock head.

The room spun as the warning tingle became more like an explosion.

At the last second Max had a moment of clarity and reached out to somehow try and pull Jordan's mouth off his dick.

She protested and he lost the battle. Her fingers gripped him tight, squeezing and caressing the base of his cock as he pulsed unendingly into her mouth.

Jordan sat back on her heels and looked up at him, that sly little gleam in her eyes.

Max tried to clear his mind but one thing raged to the forefront.

"Where the fuck did you learn to do that?"

Jordan felt inordinately pleased with herself. She'd nearly brought Maximillian to his knees.

Why did the name Maximillian sound like someone who should run in her family's circle? And, ew, why was she thinking about them? They were the last thing she wanted to think of at the moment. Not when she had a hot, willing, sexy man at her disposal.

She grabbed his hand, intent on pulling him down the darkened hallway toward her bedroom, only to get yanked to a stop.

"Pants around the knees, kamikaze. When I trip, we'll be lying on the floor instead of in your bed."

"Then take them off."

His eyes widened a fraction of an inch and when she looked down she saw that his cock had responded in kind, only way more than a fraction.

"Time's a wastin'," she taunted, licking her lips and staring at his erection. She could certainly go for round two right where

172

they were.

"Fuck."

"You say that a lot. Care to put an action to the word?" She sidled back to him and kissed his open mouth.

His hands cradled her face and angled her head right where he wanted her, then he took over the kiss. His tongue plunged deep. With the toe of her shoe, she pressed down on the crotch of his jeans and pushed them to the floor.

Jordan broke the kiss and once again kneeled on the floor.

"Jordan..." Max's voice held a warning. Jordan chuckled and glanced up at him.

"Relax, big guy. Just helping you out of your shoes and pants."

"Oh." His shoulders slumped and she swore a look of disappointment flashed across his face.

She smiled and bent to the task of unlacing his shoes, pulling them off his feet, followed by his socks, which he helped with by standing on one foot when needed, then yanked his jeans off too. That done, she jumped to her feet, grabbed the hem of his shirt and relieved him of it also, leaving him standing at her front door deliciously naked.

A round, puckered scar on his right side, about bellybutton height, attracted her attention. Her fingertips reached for it as if uncontrolled. His hand wrapped around hers, keeping her from touching.

"What happened?" It sure as hell looked nasty, whatever it was.

Max brought her fingers to his lips and placed a soft kiss on each knuckle.

"It's old. Nothing to think about now."

She shrugged it off. "I'm all for thinking about other things."

"That's good. Now get your ass in that bedroom of yours and strip."

Jordan sucked in a breath. Her nipples tightened against the silk of her bra. Though she'd decided to go it alone, away from the money and out of her parents' clutches, at this precise moment in time she was never happier that she'd continued purchasing her expensive lingerie. Nipples against smooth, satiny silk versus nipples against cheap, discount cotton—silk won hands down.

She turned and sashayed down the hall, looking back over her shoulder with the best come-fuck-me eyes she could muster.

Max's gaze narrowed and his cock bobbed before leading him like a man on a leash toward her.

In her bedroom, she flicked on the light then stopped at the foot of the bed and surveyed the room. At least she hadn't left it a complete disaster when she'd hastily refreshed and changed her outfit before heading to the bar earlier.

"Didn't I say to strip?"

Jordan's heart pounded and her pussy clenched. This was exactly what she'd wanted, right? With slow deliberation, she turned and began unbuttoning her shirt, letting him see each inch of skin uncovered as she did so. This time he licked his lips. She loved the way his nostrils flared and a tiny muscle ticked in his jaw.

When she'd gotten her shirt all the way undone, it fell from her arms to the floor, and she reached for the button on her jeans. Two steps brought him into her personal space and a slap of his hand on her wrists wrenched the material from her hands.

"I changed my mind. I want to do this part myself. After all, you divested me of mine."

"Whatever you say." *Whatever makes you get inside me that much quicker.*

Long, lean fingers of one hand dipped behind the waistband while the other hand lowered the zipper with a hiss. Then both hands went to the small of her back, delved beneath her panties and pushed the fabric of both materials over her rear end and down to her knees before he cupped her cheeks and squeezed. Hugging her close, he nibbled on her earlobe, drawing a ragged breath from her lungs. His cock nestled at her tummy when she wanted it lower. Time to take the bull by the horns.

"Unless you plan on fucking my bellybutton, we need to be in a better position."

"Greedy imp."

"Hey, you already got some action. I'm the one still unsatisfied here."

Those long fingers wandered from the crack of her ass to the slick opening of her vagina and one, maybe two of them entered her. Her head dropped back and her eyes rolled.

"Tight." He half-growled, half-groaned the word in her ear.

Imagine that. A couple years of sexual abstinence had made her a born-again virgin.

His tongue licked a path up her neck and back down to the V at her throat. With his unoccupied hand, the one not currently making her heart race, Max bent her backward and suckled a nipple through the silk barrier.

Holy freakin' God.

The upside-down view of her dresser reminded her of condoms. Did she have any in that drawer that weren't dry and cracked from age? Did he have any? Was she destined not to get any nookie after all? The mere thought made her want to puke. Sheer bliss sat within reach and she might not achieve it.

"Do you have a condom?" she blurted, still hanging upside down.

He snickered. "Just one?" His fingers retreated from her pussy and she nearly whimpered.

"Well. For starters." *At least.* Two or three might be better.

"I think I got us covered," he whispered, moving to the other nipple.

"Can you possibly do that without the bra in the way?"

"I'm getting to it. Patience, kamikaze."

"Why do you keep calling me that?" She squeezed the back of his neck when he bit down gently on her nipple.

"That damn bike."

She jerked her head up and stared at him. "But, wait. You called me that *before* you saw my bike."

For a split second she swore his eyes widened. "I saw you pull in to the parking lot of the bar. Kamikaze was the first thought that came to mind."

"Hmm. Well, you're going to have to get over your insecurities about my bike."

"Oh yeah?"

She nodded. "I would hate to think you think I'm a fragile little butterfly because that would mean you might hold back with me in this bed right here behind me and then I would have to hurt you, and while I'm not opposed to strangling the woman in the bathroom, I don't want to hurt you before I'm done with you."

One of his eyebrows rose to an impressive height. He turned her and nudged her onto the bed, stripping off her jeans and panties as she went, leaving her only in the bra, wet circles from his mouth surrounding the taut buds.

"You wanted to strangle someone?"

He spread her legs apart, exposing her pussy, which she was sure glistened in the overhead light. He looked at her core like a starving tiger eyeing a fat water buffalo. "Can we talk about this later?"

"Yep." He flicked the closure of the bra between her breasts and removed the offending item, then kneeled between her feet.

His hot breath fanned over her pussy a second before his tongue touched her clit. Her feet didn't quite reach the floor so she had nothing to brace herself against. Those fingers returned, stroking her channel, while his tongue flicked and lapped at the bundle of nerves, driving her insane.

Jordan propped herself on her elbows and watched. His gaze caught and held hers, seeming to dare her to come. An outcome which was quickly approaching fruition. She couldn't remember the last time she'd come so soon. Normally she had to really work at what she knew would be her one and only release. Hell, sometimes after working it forever she still never came. Then it was time to bring on the fake. While some men didn't give a rat's ass if they got their woman off or not, there were a few out there whose ego got severely offended if they didn't. She'd learned it was best to fake it either way if she didn't come.

Maximillian, however, seemed to be having no trouble bringing her clit great pleasure.

Her thighs shook where she tried to grip the edge of the bed, and she dug her heels into the bedframe for a miniscule amount of leverage.

Then his fingers touched something inside her, causing her back to arch and stars to flicker behind her eyelids. Had she ever actually seen stars before? His mouth closed on her clit, sucking the tiny nub behind his teeth and biting ever so slightly. The small pressure was all it took for the lingering tingle of anticipation to explode into throb after throb of long-awaited ecstasy. This was what she'd hoped for. This and more.

Max kissed her clit, sending a subsequent frisson of leftover orgasm through her, then moved up her body, pushing her farther back on the bed. He settled over her, his erection nestled against her pussy, and she couldn't for the life of her figure out why she'd ever waited so long to get back in the game.

"You're beautiful when you come."

Well, what could she say to that?

"If I get up, do you promise to stay right here in this position until I get back?"

She lifted her head, panicking with the idea he might run

out on her before the big finale. It didn't matter that she was done and wouldn't likely see the stars again for another two or three years, she wanted to feel him inside her. "Where are you going?"

Hadn't she given him good head? Had she offended him somehow?

"Condoms. In the jeans you stripped off me at the front door."

"Oh."

His mouth descended on hers, transferring her body's taste to her lips. "Don't move."

"Couldn't if I tried."

"I heard that," he called, disappearing into the dark hall of her apartment. "Son of bitch."

Jordan bucked upright. "What's wrong?"

"Stubbed my toe."

A crash sounded down the hall and another curse that sounded something like "fuck me" and "shit". Jordan cringed and smiled at the same time.

"I am so sorry. Whatever it is, I'll replace it." His voice carried down the length of the hall.

She sort of doubted he'd be able to. If she was right about his vicinity, he'd probably knocked over the Tiffany stained-glass lamp she'd received as a house-warming gift from her best friend who couldn't imagine Jordan living a life without all the things money could buy. It *had* fit so perfectly with the rest of her décor and getting rid of it would have hurt Phoebe's feelings so she'd left it.

"Don't worry about it." From her best friend or not, it was still only an object. Not important in the grand scheme of life. Certainly not as important as a best friend.

Her mother wouldn't agree, but then that's one of the reasons Jordan had moved out of her parents' smothering mansion and lifestyle to pursue her own dreams. Her owning a dance studio was definitely not in their plans. They wanted her to settle down with whomever they chose and become a high-society wife and mother with all the social status that entailed.

No child of hers was going to grow up raised by a nanny and a tutor.

Max's grumbling grew closer as did her renewed interest in what her very near future held.

And then the whole place went dark.

"What the hell?"

"Max?" Jordan sat up.

"Your lights went out."

She giggled. "I can see that. Come back to bed."

"Let me check this out first."

"Don't bother. It's happened several times before. Something about the breaker. I can fix it later. Much later..."

"Are you sure?"

"Yes, Max."

"Fine. Talk to me so I can find you in this tomb."

She tried for her sexiest voice. "I'm over here, Max." She even pouted and batted her eyelashes, though the effect was lost since he couldn't see her.

The bed shook and Max cursed again. "Son of a bit—"

"Get down here before you mangle yourself or break something else."

"Jesus. I really am sorry. I'll replace it, I promise."

Great. Now she'd have to find some cheap knock-off brand so he wouldn't feel guilty about breaking the lamp she really didn't put much monetary value on anyway. It was pretty, yes, but people meant more to her than things any day.

She wondered for a split second how Max viewed relationships, then shook her head of the notion. One night was all she was likely to get from Maximillian. She didn't even know his last name, for chrissake. Then again, he didn't know hers either. And since she didn't go by her real last name, he wouldn't know her from any other Jane Doe. "There's only one thing I want from you, Max."

"Pushy."

"That's right. Now, can you see to get that condom on or do you need some help?"

"Please tell me you're not serious," he groused.

"Only trying to be of service." And she was practically dying waiting on him.

"I'll show you service."

Oh, please do. Please!

The bed dipped between her legs and Max fitted his body on top of hers, the head of his cock snuggling right where she wanted it to.

"Yes." She threw her head back and begged him to thrust into her.

"I'll go as slow as I want, kamikaze."

The tip of his erection penetrated her opening. His arms came down on either side of her shoulders to hold his weight, which caused the smattering of his chest hair to tickle her nipples.

Max's hips flexed, filling more of her with his cock. Jordan bent her knees and squeezed her thighs against his waist.

"You're killing me, Jordan."

"Yes I will if you don't start fucking me, *Max.*"

He thrust forward, impaling her on his hard length, making her gasp at the sudden fullness and the slight pain.

"Breathe, Jordan." His thumbs traced a line down either side of her face. She hadn't even known she wasn't breathing.

The air left her lungs with a whoosh.

"Am I hurting you?"

She shook her head, then realized he couldn't see her. "No."

"Good." He withdrew, the action setting off a riot of

sensation in her pussy and unbelievably making her clit tingle again as if it were revving up for another climax. Impossible, she knew, but she wasn't about to argue when it felt so damn good.

In and out he thrust. She'd never felt so high from sex. Like it was the greatest thing on earth. With each entry he did something, some kind of twist of his hips that pushed against her clit. A drop of sweat landed on her forehead, mixing with her own.

The tension grew at her pussy, the almost-there impression that she might come again. His body rocked into hers as if he knew exactly how to wring every ounce of a second climax from her. But it wasn't enough. Frustration hit her like a sledgehammer to the back of head. So close. So close.

His fingers slipped into the curls surrounding her hidden bundle of nerves and caressed her.

"Shiiit."

"Come for me, Jordan. Come *with* me."

"Yes, yes, yes, yes, yes." She wanted to so bad. So bad it hurt. Seriously. A cramp seized her calf where she held it so rigidly against his thigh.

Jordan cried out in both pain and astonishment as the first wave of an orgasm broke over her.

After thrusting one last time, Max went still above her, his own release pulsing within her.

For the first time in her entire life, Jordan wished there was no latex barrier involved. She wanted to know what it felt like to have a man's semen spurt into her. This man's sperm.

Her heart pounded in revelation. She knew nothing about Max. Not even his last name. And she wanted him without protection?

What in the hell was wrong with her?

The cramp became more charley horse and bit into her leg with ferocious strength, destroying any sense of post-climactic euphoria there might have been.

"Charley horse, charley horse," she cried, squirming beneath Max in an effort to reach the afflicted muscle.

"Shit. Where?" Max withdrew from her pussy and rolled to her side.

"Calf."

He grabbed her leg.

"The other one," she gasped, pinching her eyes closed against the insane pain. Max took hold of it and rubbed up and down her calf, feeling for the bunched muscle and massaging it with absolute accuracy.

Once she was able to breathe again, she wilted into the bed.

"Better?"

"Yes. Thank you."

"No problem." He continued stroking her leg from knee to ankle.

"I'm sorry I ruined it."

"You didn't ruin anything, kamikaze. I think the top of my head blew off."

"Gross. I can't wait to see that mess when the lights come back on."

"You said this happens a lot?"

"Yeah. Old place. The breaker pops. It just needs to be flipped, I'm sure. Been doing it every once in awhile since I moved in."

His lips touched her shoulder and moved to the tip of her breast. "And how long has that been?"

"Three..." she gulped when his mouth closed around the nipple and the rest of her sentence came out in a squeak, "...years or so."

Max wrapped his tongue around the sweet berry in his

mouth. He loved her taste, her squeaks when she came, the way her body arched beneath him. In the past he'd been one to have some fun and then run, but right now he wanted nothing more than to wrap her in his arms and snuggle under the covers. He imagined waking up next to her in the morning and slipping inside her tight sheath while she came awake.

He slid his hand down her abdomen and into the nest of curls shielding her mound and found himself wanting to go another round right now. Fuck waiting until morning.

Max slipped his fingers down the cream heating her slit. Jordan's back arched, bringing her breast up and farther into his mouth. He couldn't get enough of her. His cock responded as well, ready for another go of her pussy pulsing around him. He loved her smell and her attitude and her—

Son of a fucking bitch, Jensen. You know nothing about her. She's a night of good sex. Not wife material.

As soon as he thought it, he nearly jumped off the bed.

Since when did a round of sex—albeit utterly fanfuckingtastic sex—make him think in terms of a wife?

With one last glide of his fingers through her core, Max untangled himself and stood.

"Where are you going?" She sounded almost frightened. Because she thought he was leaving her or because she was scared of the dark?

"To clean up first, then I'm going to go fix your lights."

"Aw, my hero."

"Yep, that's me." He flexed his arms in a superhero pose then lowered them when he realized the effect was lost in the dark.

Max was beginning to wonder who Jordan really was. She lived in a moderate apartment, had a job that surely didn't pay a ton—although she had mentioned another job so he guessed she did all right. She had to be if she had the kind of money he now needed to replace the Tiffany lamp he'd dumped on the floor and allowed to shatter into a million pieces. His mother had enough of the damn things in the home he'd grown up in that he'd known as soon as he'd seen the colorful light shade that it had been a Tiffany.

Of course she could have inherited the item, in which case he felt like an even bigger moron.

And she was probably wondering how the hell he was going to pay for such an extravagant item.

Nevertheless, it would give him the chance to see her again.

He turned and felt his way to the bathroom he'd seen to the right, hoping to God he didn't stub another toe or worse, cause the Waterford vase he'd observed to come off the dresser next to the door. That's all he needed, to be into her for another grand on top of the Tiffany. Not that he couldn't afford it, he just didn't want her feeling guilty for thinking he couldn't.

He made his way to the sink and over to the toilet.

"Trashcan's between the toilet and sink," she said, right behind him, making him come out of his skin.

Some security specialist. He cleared his throat. "Thank you."

After disposing of the condom and washing his hands he worked his way back out. Now, though, he could see a minute amount, mainly her silhouette in the doorway. There was a glow behind her.

"Where is that light coming from?" He put his hands on her shoulders and turned her to face the illumination.

"The street, I guess. I opened the blinds because I saw it coming through the cracks."

"Why are the streetlights on but not the build...? Never mind. Your breaker wouldn't make all the lights in the neighbor—"

A crash of glass breaking interrupted him. Max shoved Jordan behind his back and put himself between her and the bedroom doorway. Someone was breaking into her apartment and Max had no clothes on. Even more disturbing was the fact that his gun was out in the car where'd he'd left it so Jordan wouldn't discover it and ask questions.

"Get in the closet and stay there until I tell you to come out," he murmured. Jordan shivered behind him, her hands fisted at his shoulder blades.

"What the hell do you think you're going to do?"

"My job." Anything and everything to protect her. The lights going out and someone breaking in wasn't a coincidence.

"What kind of job do you have? Cop?"

"Something like that." He shoved her toward the closet door, thankful he'd absorbed the layout of the room when he'd entered.

"You can't go out there naked," she insisted quietly, pushing something soft into his hands. It felt like a robe of some kind. Damn him for leaving his phone attached to the waistband of his pants which were still out in the foyer.

"Call nine-one-one from your phone and stay the hell hidden."

There was a soft curse from the front room and the crunching of glass. Their uninvited guest had just found the Tiffany.

"Hide *now*." Fuck the robe. Max was going into battle Highlander style, sans clothes.

He tiptoed to the door and heard Jordan mutter, "Stupid fool." A half-inch-wide beam of light illuminated the Tiffany glass. The shards sparkled from the hardwood, then the beam swept away. Whoever the perp was, he wasn't after Jordan for the moment. Max would make sure it stayed that way.

A black-clad figure complete with mask trailed the light to a desk in the far corner of the TV room. The light disappeared for a second behind the intruder then reappeared on the opposite side of the desk. The squeaking of the chair when the man pushed it out of the way was followed by another muttered curse.

He flicked through the papers on the desk, almost negligently causing them to flutter to the ground, then laid the pencil holder on its side, letting the pencils fall out.

What the hell? Something was way off.

Next the man moved to the couch and threw a pillow to the floor. There was no freaking purpose to the man's movements. They were totally random.

At the coffee table he slid the magazines off and shoved the whole table out of whack. The cushions on the couch were the next to fall to his careful disheveling.

The man was trying to make it look like someone had ransacked the place.

Furthermore, though he was being quiet, he didn't exactly seem worried about getting caught, so he either didn't think the occupant of the apartment was home or hoped she was asleep, which didn't seem too likely considering it wasn't exactly the dead of night or anything.

Max crept his way along the wall, careful not to reveal himself until he could get close enough. Unfortunately the Tiffany had spread out farther than he thought. It crackled beneath his bare foot, cutting into his skin. Max hissed.

The man looked up, his widened eyes eerily lit up through the slit in the mask by the flashlight. He sprang from his seat and shot through the doorway leading to the kitchen. Max stepped on more glass while giving chase.

"Son of a bitch." A door slammed. No way in hell would Max catch up. Not naked and sporting glass in his feet.

"Is he gone?" Jordan's voice made him turn around from where he stood staring at the dark door.

"I thought I told you to hide."

She snorted. "As if. You're in the buff and barefoot, in case you hadn't noticed. I wasn't going to let you chase some maniac like that."

A strong light flicked on, making him squint in its brightness.

"Found a flashlight and called the police. They're on their way so you might want to think about putting some clothes on before they get here." She shined the light on the floor and pointed out his pants and shirt.

Max hobbled over to them, pissed off. A woman coming to his rescue when she should still be nestled inside some hidey-hole.

"What's wrong?"

"Stepped on the glass I broke earlier. Be careful, it's right where you're standing."

"That's why I put shoes on." She moved closer to him where he sat after gathering his clothes. "Let me see."

"It's nothing."

"Let me see, macho man."

"Fine." He lifted one foot so she could see the bottom.

"Shit. Don't put the shoes on. I've got to go get some tweezers." She turned back the way she came. "Or maybe a pair of pliers."

In the dark once more, Max was left to wonder who the hell had broken in and why. Then again, the woman had Tiffany and Waterford so there was no telling what else she had. Which made him want to get up and investigate.

Also made him want to put a fist through the man's face for daring to enter her residence.

Just what the hell was going on?

Chapter Five

The lights were still off when the police arrived. Max could have gone outside to investigate, but he wasn't willing to leave Jordan alone, and with the police minutes away, he'd cooled his heels and waited. He was happy to see the officer who entered was someone he knew.

"Simmons." Max shook the officer's hand and gestured him inside. He left the door open so they might see better in the spill of light from the street. It aided the glow of candles Jordan had lit in the last few minutes while waiting for the police.

"What're you doing here, Jensen?"

"You two know each other?" Jordan paused in sweeping the shards of glass into a dustpan.

"Yes," Max answered her, then turned his attention back to Simmons. "I was with Ms...Jordan, when this went down."

Officer Simmons looked down at Max's hastily wrapped feet. "What happened to your feet?"

Max pointed to the floor littered with the glass. "I knocked over the lamp earlier then stepped all over it when I was chasing the suspect out."

Simmons's right eyebrow rose impressively. "You were barefoot? So I'm guessing this wasn't a professional call."

Jordan spoke before Max could. "Yes. He was barefoot. Now you've probably gathered that we were sleeping together so can we just get on with why someone broke into my apartment?"

Simmons' other eyebrow rose to meet the first. "Absolutely. When did the lights first go off?"

Jordan cocked her head to the side in thought. Good thing she seemed to know because apart from the throb in his toe from kicking the damn table and then the mind-blowing sex, Max wasn't sure he would have been able to tell Simmons if an elephant had been dancing in the room.

"Mmm...maybe thirty minutes or so ago."

Simmons nodded, stuffed the small Maglite under his chin so he could see and wrote the time down in a little notebook he pulled from his pocket. "I checked. Electricity is only out in this apartment. Rest of the complex is on. My partner's out checking the box right now. The caller told the dispatcher the perp was gone. We've got a unit cruising, looking for anybody out of place. Doubt we'll find anyone though."

Simmons surveyed the room. "Tell me what happened."

"We were in the bedroom." No use hiding anything now that Jordan had outed them with her first breath. "Heard glass breaking. I told Jordan to hide in the closet then I tiptoed down the hall. I saw a black shape and the beam of a flashlight, like a mini. He went straight for the desk in the corner." He stabbed a thumb over his shoulder in the direction of the desk. "Kind of rooted around for a bit, tipped over the pencil holder, moved the cushions on the couch. If he was looking for something, he sure didn't seem to be in a hurry to do it. It was more a methodical ransacking. I couldn't figure out what the hell he was doing. I'd have gotten to him except I stepped on the damn glass and alerted him. He bolted before I could get across the mess and went out the door."

"You armed?"

"Armed?" Jordan's voice went a couple octaves higher than normal. "He was naked, where would he have been armed? Furthermore, *why* would he have been?"

The lights flicked on, surprising them.

Max took her hand in his and ignored the naked remark.

189

The last thing he needed was to hear the backlash of having chased an intruder naked. "No. It's in the car."

"Does she not know what you do?" Simmons seemed shocked as he directed the question at Max.

"No."

Jordan yanked her hand from Max's. "What do you do?"

"Max is a security expert."

Damn Simmons.

"A security expert, huh? Well no wonder you know people." Now her tone had dropped. "Why didn't you tell me? Wait a minute. Did my *mother* send you? Is that what this is about?"

If looks could kill, Max was pretty sure either he or Jordan's mother was about to die.

"Now hold on. I don't know your mother, so no she didn't send me, and I didn't tell you because it never really came up. I don't know what *you* do either." Well, not everything she did anyway. He didn't think she'd be very happy about his finding her while he watched one of his cases. God knew how she'd react if she discovered he'd followed her all over town.

The point he was getting at was that neither of them had shared any personal information beyond their first names.

"Touché." She sort of deflated and returned her attention back to the mess.

Why did he feel like he'd just gotten kicked in the gut?

"Ma'am, can you think of any reason someone might want to break in?"

When she glanced at Simmons, her face was once again composed. In fact, Max could almost swear her eyes glittered with anger. Had to be a trick of the light.

"No. Well. Yes. I guess. Maybe. Not realistically, but theoretically? Maybe."

"Jordan."

She whipped her head his direction. "What?"

"Breathe." He stood behind her, rested his hands on her shoulders and gave her a squeeze, trying hard to ignore the tremor that went through her body. She seemed more nervous now than she had when a stranger had been in her home, and Max's protective nature went on high alert.

She lifted her chin and spoke to the officer. "My name is Jordan Landon."

Max dropped his hands and stared at the back of Jordan's head. It couldn't be.

"Okay." Simmons scribbled on his pad.

"Then I guess there's a few multimillion reasons someone might break into your place." Max gritted his teeth. Why in the hell was the heiress to Landon Holdings living in an apartment? And where the fuck was her security? He sure hoped to shit she didn't count a flimsy door lock as security.

Her spine went ramrod straight, and if it were possible for fire to actually shoot from one's ears, it would be doing so right now from hers.

"Excuse me?" Simmons shifted his weight to his other foot.

"Ms. Landon is Jordan Grace Landon, heiress to Landon Holdings," Max said softly.

Jordan's eyes narrowed, but he had no clue why she was angry at him.

"Oh." This from Simmons who suddenly looked a little awestruck.

Jordan's hands landed on her hips and her lips thinned. "I'll have you know that I have lived here for three years without one problem and the first time I bring a man here..." she was slowly turning toward him, "...all of a sudden someone breaks in." She stabbed her finger into his chest, and he grunted but took the semi-onslaught. "Maybe it's you they ought to be investigating. Maybe you were sent by someone to keep me occupied while another person went through my things."

Max captured her finger to keep it from poking him any

further and pulled her flush to his body.

"Kamikaze, if I'd been sent to keep you occupied, I wouldn't have lost my mind after seeing you naked and sent a priceless Tiffany lamp to the floor."

She sucked in a shocked breath. "You knew that was Tiffany?"

"Baby, we roll in the same circles. Yes, I knew it was Tiffany and I *will* replace it, I swear. As for the rest of this conversation, can we have it away from Officer Simmons' ears?"

Jordan appeared as if she'd rather stick a hot poker in his eye but nodded. He kissed her lips because he simply couldn't resist. Jordan, however, had no problem resisting him, and kept that beautiful mouth of hers sealed.

"So..." Simmons' gaze went back and forth between Max and Jordan.

"No, there's no one in particular I can think of off the top of my head who might want to break in." She sounded tired, as if she just wanted the whole mess to disappear. He couldn't blame her.

"Then again..." She cocked her head to the side, then those eyes narrowed again and her mouth pursed.

"Who?" The question was echoed by both Max and Simmons.

"Dirk Clement."

"Who the hell is Dirk Clement?" Max couldn't contain the possessive growl that slipped out.

"I clean his house." Her face contorted, and Max had a sneaking suspicion it was with disgust.

Max's first thought was to look the man up as soon as Simmons left, and his second was he couldn't wait to see the man with a black eye.

Jordan seethed inside and wondered just what the hell was going on. One minute she was a pole-dancing instructor trying to earn enough money to open her business, the next she was sleeping with a security specialist. Someone exactly the type her mother would plant to keep an eye on her.

Ooh, that woman was going to get an earful. The last thing Jordan needed was another babysitter.

And Max? Goddamn it. The man had taken his duties to the next level, hadn't he? Sleeping with her? She guessed he at least got out of it whatever her mother had paid him.

The whole idea made her feel sleazier than Dirk Clement ever had. At least Dirk had nothing to do with her mother. Clement had his own nefarious reasons. He'd been trying to worm his way into her bed in the utmost of immoral fashions. Hadn't he been trying to do that since the moment he'd hired her? But break into her apartment?

Jordan shivered in revulsion. Gross. Absolutely gross.

She seethed in silence, waiting for Max to return from walking Officer Simmons out. She'd had the most fantastic sex of her life a short while ago, and now the man who'd revved her body might have been a plant. He'd said he didn't know her mother. A lie? Dare she believe him after all the other stupid stunts her family had pulled since she'd moved out?

He had looked shocked when she'd given them her name. Then again, if was being paid, he'd probably do whatever he needed to keep up the charade.

She needed a shower. And she wanted to see his face right before she slammed the door on it.

Except she wasn't sure it was possible to forget the things Max had done to her. Her traitorous body for sure wanted a repeat. And she for damn sure wanted answers. Now.

Damn it all to hell.

The door clicked open and in he walked like some kind of god. Even though she was good and pissed at both Max and Dirk Clement, nothing could detract from Max's looks or the way he made her heart race at the mere sight of him. It had been that way since she'd first seen him at the bar.

He shut the door and she was damn glad to see an expression of resignation on his face. She hoped to hell this wasn't going to be easy on him.

"Well?" she started, ready to get on with it.

He shrugged. "The patrols didn't spot anything unusual."

"Not what I'm talking about Maximillian *Jensen.*" Then it dawned on her. With all her stewing, she hadn't put the names together earlier when the officer had recognized Max. "Jensen. As in...Kara Patterson-Jensen? You're her son?"

"Yes," he admitted, not looking the least bit sorry.

"So how did...?" So damn confused. And even more damning. They did run in the same circles, and Max was exactly the type of man her mother would hire.

"Shall we sit or hash this out standing up?" Max stuck his hands in his pockets.

"As long as you stay on your side of the couch and don't touch me."

His eyes narrowed dangerously. "I don't think I can agree to that, kamikaze."

Jordan crossed her arms over her chest.

Standoff.

Max didn't move, just stood there looking all sexy and determined.

"For God's sake. Let's get it over with." She actually harrumphed.

He nodded sharply. "There are better things we could be doing."

"Not a chance, bucko."

"So you say."

Jordan replaced the cushions then sat on one end of her cream-colored microfiber couch. She realized her mistake a second too late. Max sat next to her, not giving her an inch, and since she'd foolishly believed he'd be a gentleman and sit at the other end, she didn't have any room to breathe, let alone move. He grabbed her hand and held tight when she tried to pull it back.

Brute.

"I never meant for us to make love."

She snorted. "Little late for that revelation." And why in the hell did his announcement break her heart?

"We really should have never even met." His thumb played lazily over the pulse point at her wrist in an almost hypnotic fashion.

"Start at the beginning. And try not to leave anything out," she said, deadpan.

He...squirmed, for lack of a better word, with an air of discomfort. "First, are you sleeping with this Dirk Clement?"

"What?" Jordan leapt from her seat and stared at him incredulously. "That is seriously nasty, and why in the hell would you ever think that? How do you even know the scumbag?"

His shoulders dropped in relief. "Thank God."

She thought that was what he said. She couldn't be sure because he muttered it.

"I don't know him. Just made me jealous."

She couldn't stop the gag that choked her. "Jealous? That's rich."

He smiled. "Yes. Jealous. I had a hunch you didn't like him based on your expression, but I had to know for sure. I was beginning to think I might have to kill the man for touching you."

"Fine, get on with it. I want to know what's going on. How much is my mother paying you?"

"Nothing. I told you. I don't know your mother. The truth is—"

"The truth. Right."

"—that I was following one of your students."

"Students?"

"Yes."

Jordan shook her head. "One of my...my aerobics class?" Complete confusion took over.

"Yep." Max sat back and locked his hands behind his head. The action drew her gaze to his chest.

Jordan swallowed.

"Annie Devlin."

"Annie? Annie who never speaks and covers up with a full-length fur so that no one sees her, Annie?"

"Uh, yeah, her."

"What do you want with her? And what the hell did this have to do with me?"

"I was hired by her husband because of her secret rendezvous on Friday nights. Imagine my surprise when what I found was your sweet little body wrapped around a pole."

Jordan gasped. "You were watching me?"

"No, I was watching her. But the second I realized Mrs. Devlin wasn't having an affair, well, then my attention turned to you."

"Well, isn't that special." She didn't have a clue what else to say. "So you weren't hired by my mother?"

"No."

"Then how is it you ended up at the same bar as me?"

Max sighed. "Sit down."

Jordan must have hesitated a bit too long because his arm snaked out and he grabbed her, pulled her onto his lap and wrapped his arms around her.

"Much better." His murmur tickled her ear and sent a shiver down her spine. He might as well have licked her pussy. "I admit to following you."

"What the hell for?"

"You've got to be kidding me, Jordan. One look at you in your little class and I was drooling. Then you came out and got on that damn bike and I just about had a coronary."

Realization dawned. "That's why you were calling me kamikaze."

"Yes. I swear if I ever see you on that hunk of metal again, it'll be too soon."

"Hunk of metal? You really should be nicer to my baby. I love him."

"Anyway... After you got to the bar I thought, 'I can't leave her there. What if she drinks too much then gets back on that stupid contraption?' So I stayed despite wondering if I'd lost my mind."

Dang it, she wanted to believe him, but wow. Seriously? Then again, how else would the man know Annie's name?

Um, hello? Security specialist. He probably knew more about her than she did.

Max frowned. "You don't believe me." His hand rubbed a small circle on her back. Then he shifted her, forcing her legs to straddle his thighs. The position put her breasts right at mouth level for him. Her nipples peaked in response, damn them.

She deflated. "I'm starting to," she said begrudgingly. She shouldn't still want him. Not with all the doubts she had. But she had a feeling his activities beyond his initial surveillance of her were not something he typically partook of. Feeling impish, she walked her fingers up his chest. "So...do you sleep with all your suspects?"

"You aren't a suspect. Or anyone of interest. At least not of criminal interest." His grin told her she was of interest in another way though. He swallowed. "I should fire myself for stalking you and doing what I did to you."

"Did *to* me? You're over-thinking it. You hardly forced yourself on me. I'm sure I was quite the willing participant. In

197

fact, if you're telling the truth, then *I* was the one who picked *you* up at the bar."

He grabbed her fingers as she slowly inched them down to the hardness she felt growing against the apex of her thighs.

"Still, it was completely unethical, immoral—"

"Yadda, yadda, yadda. We did nothing wrong or unethical, immoral or illegal. We were strangers who picked each other up at a bar. I won't tell anyone if you won't."

"Why aren't you married? And why the *hell* are you without protection?" He blurted the question and she saw that he couldn't believe he'd asked.

"I'm sure my mother has some Kennedy picked out and waiting in the wings for me." She watched Max's lip curl in distaste. Or jealousy, she couldn't decide. "Her idea of a future and mine don't mesh."

His hands went to her bottom and pulled her closer to his body, rubbing his denim-covered length along her slit. She wished she hadn't put the pants on, but then meeting the police without pants might have been a tad strange.

"Our mothers must be related." His lips went to her throat and teased the sensitive skin.

"Why's...why's that?" Her clit sat up and begged for more attention than it was getting.

"I'm pretty sure mine has a Rockefeller all picked out for me."

"Aw, that's sweet."

"How are you involved with Clement?" His thumb pressed on her sweet spot, making her eyes roll.

She arched back, seeking better contact. "I told you. I'm his cleaning lady."

Max grasped her shoulders and shook her once. She focused on his face. "My next question then is why is Jordan Grace Landon cleaning houses?"

His words wounded her. Jordan jerked out of his hold and

off his lap. "I guess you wouldn't know a damn thing about wanting something so badly you could taste it."

He snorted. "I did want something really bad and it tasted fantastic. It's part of the reason we're having this conversation in the first place."

"I wasn't talking about sex." She ground her teeth in frustration. The last thing she needed was for him to condemn her reasons for making it on her own.

"You and I both know what we did wasn't sex."

Jordan sniffed and turned her shoulder. She had thought it had been more, but now with the jumble of thoughts in her head... Had he played her like a million-dollar fiddle or were they really just two people attracted to one another?

"What is it you want so bad you'd live outside of the protection your family can provide? I'm not judging you, Jordan, I'm curious." He eyed the apartment for a long moment, and anger boiled in her stomach.

Please God, don't let him be like her parents.

Jordan let out a harsh breath and sank onto the couch again. "I want to buy my own dance studio. It's all I've ever wanted to do. While my mother thought ballet dancing was fine for poise, no way in hell would she allow me to do something so menial. I left. To prove to her I don't need her money to live a meaningful life."

"Now I know our mothers are related."

She couldn't help but smile. "That would be a bit squicky because that would make us related. What did she do?"

"Definitely don't want to be related. I left too, though I did use some of her money to start my security business. I'm the black sheep of the family," he said proudly.

Everything in her eased. She cuddled into his side. "Well then, we're quite the pair, aren't we?"

His thumb traced a lazy circle on her shoulder. "I like the sound of that."

Jordan's nipples pebbled and a funny twist went through her belly. First, though, she still had to deal with who had broken into her home.

"Why did he come here?"

"I don't know. But I intend to find out. Any idea what whoever he was would be looking for on your desk?"

"No clue."

"I didn't get the feeling he was doing anything other than trying to make it look like he'd been searching for something."

"But why?"

"Well, let's go see then, shall we? Won't hurt to see if I'm wrong." He pushed up and then pulled her to her feet before dragging her to the desk.

There were papers strewn across the top, papers that had been organized pre break-in. She sat down, blew a few strands of hair off her face and tucked them behind her ears. She really needed a ponytail holder.

"Unless it was small, I'm pretty sure he didn't have anything in his hands besides a flashlight when he bolted."

Jordan pushed some of the papers around, trying to remember what had been there in the first place. A class schedule for the studio, her client list, a few invoices for supplies. Nothing at all interesting to a robber and certainly nothing Dirk Clement would be interested in.

"There was nothing of importance here. Anything of value I keep in a safe-deposit box or back at my mother's." She didn't see anything missing. Her gold pen still lay in its case, the crystal paperweight, the laptop, everything. "If he took anything, I can't tell."

"That's what I thought. The whole thing was just plain odd. But it was worth a shot."

They stared at each other. "So now what?" Was he going to leave? Act like nothing had happened between them? Move on to bigger and better things?

"We go to bed and deal with it in the morning."

"Excuse me?" Had she heard him right?

"I said..." he leaned over her, a hand on each arm, trapping her, "...we go to bed and deal with this in the morning."

"You're staying?"

"I can't very well leave you alone, now can I, kamikaze? You being all by yourself." He nuzzled her neck with his lips.

"Can't because someone broke into my apartment? Like you feel protective in your security-man mode, because let me tell you, those guys were another reason I left the fold." Max'd have a black eye if that was the only reason he was staying with her tonight.

"Partly. Protection is part of my job, and if you think for one second I'd leave you alone after someone got into your home, then think again. But, kamikaze..." he moved in, kissed her, deep, then pulled back, "...if I just wanted to protect you, I could call in any one of my employees to sit and watch your place for the night. Now get your ass up, your clothes off, and get into bed."

Jordan's breath stumbled in her throat. Her clit took notice, throbbing without being touched, and her nipples hardened.

"While you're getting ready, I'm going to do something about the door so we don't have any more unwelcome visitors." He straightened and walked away.

Hello? She watched the wiggle of his fantastic backside and swallowed. Had he just ordered her to do his bidding then walked off like he hadn't set her body on fire?

Hell yes he had. She leapt from the chair, scrambled around the room blowing out candles then ran down the dark hall, hoping he didn't take too long to get the door in order. The shirt she wore went flying across her room as did the panties and pants she'd donned for the police. Then she dove onto the bed, repressing the urge to scream and kick her feet like she'd just won the lottery.

A sharp pounding came from the kitchen and she envisioned him covering the hole where the intruder had broken out a pane of glass so he could reach in and unlock the door. At least the lock was still intact.

A few minutes later, right about the time her skin began to cool, Max entered her room, stripping his shirt over his head. Thank God the lights were back on because this was one show she didn't want to miss. He'd undone his jeans, leaving a gap where the head of his cock protruded. Jordan licked her lips and remembered the feeling of her mouth wrapped around it.

"Keep looking at me like that and we won't even get to the main course."

"And what is the main course?"

"You." Max stalked across the room and crawled onto the bed between her legs. His nose dipped into the crook of her knee and his lips traveled up her inner thigh before settling at her core.

"Mmm..."

His tongue flicked wildly at her clit, wasting no time in bringing her to the edge, and then a long finger penetrated her sheath and thrust in and out. This time she knew the flickering lights she saw had nothing to do with the electricity.

"Holy shit. I don't think I've ever come that quickly."

"Sorry. I couldn't wait." He suited words to action and pressed his cock head just inside her channel.

Jordan sucked in a breath, arched her back, tilting her hips to provide better access, and gripped the sheets. After that it was all about holding on for dear life while Max pounded into her. With every penetration his pelvis rubbed against her clit, jolting the fractious nerves there and keeping them from settling. His balls slapped against her anus. She'd never thought about that part of her body being erotic, but suddenly she wanted to roll over and present herself.

Max didn't give her the opportunity. He ground into her one last time and held himself rigid above her as he pulsed inside her.

Shit.

"Shit." Max echoed her thought. "I'm sorry." He put his forehead on hers. They were both breathing heavy. "Tell me you're protected."

"I can't do that."

"Damn it. Any chance you just ended your period yesterday?" He said it so hopefully she laughed out loud.

"Ah, no. Sorry."

"It's not your fault. I got wrapped up in seeing you naked and spread out for me that I didn't even think about a condom."

Jordan wrapped her arms around him, unable to hate him for a mistake. Would there be consequences? Perhaps. Would it mean the end of the world? No. She kissed his neck.

"I think it was both our faults." She lowered her tone and spoke into his ear. "Next time we'll just have to be more careful."

"I swear I've never done that before. I mean the no-condom part, not the sex. I can even show you my last physical if you want."

She laughed. "I could tell you were experienced, trust me. And ditto for me. I haven't even had sex for a while."

He lifted his head and smiled at her. "Are you sure you're not one of my mother's Rockefeller plants, brought to my attention so I'd end up getting you pregnant and then we'd have to marry?"

Jordan laughed again and crossed her heart. "As long as you promise your last name isn't really Kennedy."

"Nope." Max withdrew, leaving her feeling empty. He lay down next to her and pulled her into his arms. "Does what we're doing seem wrong?"

She played with the hairs on his chest, doing her best not

to yank them out one at a time in a nervous fit. "Nooo... Does it to you?" *Please say no. Please say no.*

"No. That's what's so scary. Everything feels so...right. Like I could get used to being with you. And since I only met you a few hours ago, you know..."

"I get it. It is a little weird, yes, but I don't regret for one second what we've done, and it isn't wrong."

Max pinched her right nipple lightly and rolled the nub between his fingers. "Definitely not wrong." He bent his head and sucked the nipple into his mouth.

After driving her crazy and making her squirm to get more, he released the bud with a pop. He nibbled his way up her breast to her collarbone, traced the length of her neck and pressed his lips to her mouth. His tongue slipped inside and danced with hers.

"Tomorrow," he said, breaking their connection, "in the light of day, we'll talk about things." He kissed her forehead and hugged her close.

It *was* late. Jordan suddenly found herself tired. She snuggled into Max's heated body and yawned. "Okay. But I warn you, I get up early."

"How early?"

"Six. Have to be at the dork's by eight."

Max turned her on her back and pushed himself up on an elbow. "The dork's?"

"Dirk Clement."

"It's Saturday."

She shrugged. "Did I mention the man was a squicky dick?"

"Squicky?" He laughed.

"Yes. It's the most appropriate word to describe him."

"Then perhaps I'll go with you and make sure he keeps his *squicky* hands off you."

"Suits me. Just be prepared to stay out of the way of my right hook, because as soon as I arrive for that job tomorrow I plan on getting fired."

Max smoothed a thumb over her cheek. "You got a good right hook, huh?"

"Years of dancing have made me very strong."

"Trust me, baby, I saw how strong you were when you were wrapped around that pole. Remind me never to piss you off. And by the way, when do I get a private showing of that little routine?"

"Hmm...you play your cards right, could be as soon as I blacken the dork's eye." She slipped her leg between his and brought it up to nudge his package. "I'll have plenty of free time afterwards."

Chapter Six

Max sat next to Jordan in her much more sensible car as they drove to Clement's estate. Jordan had gotten up earlier than she'd told him she would, waking him with a blow job and sucking him dry. Thinking about it made him get hard again. He had a feeling he was in for a lot of tight jeans in the near future. At least he'd had a change of clothes in the car with him. He'd stashed them there after getting caught once on the job without a change of clothes for three days. Now he always carried a bag.

Not that it mattered because he'd already decided he was taking Jordan back to his house after she dealt with Clement this morning. The man would be lucky to walk away with only the black eye Jordan threatened.

She pulled the car to the curb and looked at the house with a mixture of resignation and antagonism.

Dirk Clement couldn't possibly come out of this unscathed. Max had a feeling Jordan was a force to be reckoned with when pissed off. Look how far she'd gone to get out of her family's clutches.

"You mind if I go with you?"

"By all means. Be my guest." She yanked the key from the ignition and held it between her fingers like a weapon. Perhaps the dork, as Jordan referred to him, was going to lose an eye instead.

Max rocked back on his heels and waited for his knock to

be answered. The house reminded him of the one he'd grown up in. Pretentious and overdone. He wasn't sure what to expect when the door opened. A snobby butler? A maid in a French maid's costume?

Surprisingly enough, Clement himself opened the door, a sneering grin on his face which quickly turned downward when he saw Max standing next to Jordan.

"Jordan. You've brought help with you today?" His nose went into the air as he spoke.

"We need to talk, Mr. Clement." Max entered the house without being asked, pushing Clement out of the way while Jordan followed.

She got right to the heart of the matter. "Did you send someone to break into my apartment last night?"

Oh brother. Max saw Jordan's hand ball into a fist. At least she wasn't still holding her keys.

Clement's mouth opened and closed like a fish. "Absolutely not. Why on earth would you even think something like that?"

"You wanna know why?" Jordan asked, advancing on the weasel who backed up even more until his heels hit the wall behind him. "I think you're pissed because I turned you down over and over and over and this was your way of payback."

Clement's gaze shifted between Max and Jordan. "I never came on to you."

Jordan's eyes narrowed. "'Why don't you slide down here to the pool when you're finished up there, sweet thing? Care to have a drink when you're done? I can think of something much nicer for you to wear while you're working, baby.'"

Max's stomach turned and a red haze filled his vision. "You said those things to an employee?"

"That and a hundred other sordid comments." Jordan put her hands on her hips. "Did you break into my apartment?"

Clement's gaze jerked to Max's. "No. I didn't. I... No. I don't even know where you live. How could I when you wouldn't talk to me?" Sweat had started to bead on the man's forehead.

"I'm sure you have the means, Mr. Clement."

"I didn't do anything wrong." His face had turned a strange shade of purple, and Max wondered if this was what they meant in historical fiction when they said someone was suffering from apoplexy. "Fine. I said some things I shouldn't have but you..." he stabbed a finger in her direction, "...you dance around here shaking your hips and, and, try to get me all worked up. I thought you were...flirting." Clement acted as if the thought had come to him that very second. He behaved like a two-year-old who hadn't gotten his way. In short, Clement was having a temper tantrum for being caught.

"Maybe there's a reason I never told you where I live, did you ever think about that?" Jordan was definitely handling the situation better than Max thought she would. He sort of saw her now as the charging-up-the-drive-guns-blazing type. "I quit."

"You can't quit. That would be a breach of contract." Clement stamped his foot to emphasize his point.

"I'm pretty sure you breached the contract by saying the things you did. And I'm cleaning your house, not managing your money. Your contract doesn't mean much to me at the moment."

Max wished he had a pair of handcuffs. It might be nice to leave with him cuffed to the gauche fountain inside the foyer.

"It gives me great pleasure to say to your face, I quit, Mr. Clement."

"You won't get any references from me then."

Jordan turned and started walking down the steps. She spoke over her shoulder. "Your kind of references I don't need."

Max watched her leave then turned back to Clement. "If I find out you had anything to do with the break-in last night, you can be sure you'll hear from *me* again. With police in tow. And for future reference, I suggest you keep your mouth shut when the help is around unless you want a lawsuit slapped on you."

Clement vigorously nodded. "I swear. I didn't do it. I don't know where she lives."

"Let's keep it that way, shall we?"

Max didn't skip down the drive the way he wanted to, but he did whistle. One problem down, one still to go. Though they'd discovered Jordan's former employer was truly a weasel, Max still had no clue who'd broken in last night. He'd hoped the case would be solved with a visit to Clement, but despite the fact Clement was a dick, Max didn't think he'd been lying about not having anything to do with the break-in at Jordan's place.

He wondered what Jordan would say when he told her he'd be sticking to her like glue until her guest was identified, because he sure as shit didn't believe the act had been random. Someone knew who Jordan was.

Dirk Clement was an absolutely absurd man. Jordan slammed the door to her hatchback and simmered while waiting for Max. In an extremely short amount of time, she'd somehow become attached to the man. Perhaps fate, through Annie Devlin, had brought them together. She wouldn't go back in time to change things even if it meant a loan for her own studio would fall into her lap at this very moment.

Besides, she'd done some thinking during the night while she'd been pressed against Max's side. If he could use some of his family money to start his own business, perhaps she could too. Maybe she wasn't looking at things from the right angle. She was an adult. Her mother had no say in how Jordan spent her own money.

The passenger door opened, letting in a cold gust of wind.

"What an idiot." Max yanked the door closed with a thud.

"Do you think he was the one in my apartment last night?"

"No."

"Well, then who the hell...?"

He grabbed her hand and set it on his thigh. "I don't know, but you can rest assured I'll be spending the day looking into it. Are you positive you haven't pissed anyone off?"

"Positive? No."

He smiled at her which made her insides all gooey like a warm chocolate chip cookie. "Then are you sure no one knows who you are?"

"No on that account either. I don't think it would be a gigantic leap for someone to figure it out either. Apart from Dirk the dork who only thinks with his little brain." Jordan turned the key and started the engine, then pulled into the street. "You'll have to give me directions."

"I will. For now just get on 70." Max lifted Jordan's hand and kissed her knuckles.

A thrill shot through her.

The euphoric feeling got cut off by the sudden ringing of her cell phone from the cup holder. She retrieved her hand and answered the call.

As if the day couldn't get worse.

"Hello, Mother."

"Jordan, darling." Jordan rolled her eyes at her mother's sickly sweet greeting. "I've just heard about the break-in last night. Are you willing to stop playing your little game and come home now? Can't you see how dangerous it is?"

Jordan sat up. "And just how did you hear about it, Mother?" She hadn't had a chance to tell a soul yet.

"Don't be silly. Jeff, of course."

Jordan ground her teeth. "And how would Jeff know?" She hadn't seen her shadow, Jeff, since she'd flown the coop. Jordan assumed he'd been assigned some other menial job.

"You didn't honestly think I would let you run off to live in squalor, now did you? He's been watching you all along. Until now there's been no reason to interfere, but bringing home some vagrant from a bar? Jordan, really. I brought you up better than to let some common gold digger get his hands on your money. I had to do something."

"Oh. My. God. So you had someone fucking break into my place?" Jordan wanted to scream. And considering it wouldn't be very nice to kill the woman, what she really wanted to do was take a few whacks at a punching bag. Not even Dirk Clement had made her see this particular shade of red. "You've been spying on me."

"Don't you dare speak to me with such vulgarity. And yes. Someone had to stop you from squandering your life away."

Max put a calming hand on Jordan's thigh. Her cheeks heated because she had no doubt Max had heard every single word out of her mother's mouth.

"You know nothing about my life. If I want to squander every penny in my account, I'll do just that. You also know nothing about the vagrant I brought home to have wild monkey sex with all night long."

Her mother gasped and Jordan smiled, knowing she'd hit a homerun with the remark.

"Max is no vagrant, Mother. He is Kara Patterson-Jensen's son, if you must know, and even if he were a window washer you would still have no say in what or how many ways I do him."

"Jordan Grace Landon."

Jordan envisioned her mother's shocked face and kept at it. "He's the black sheep of his family too, like I am. We're a perfect pair. And...we love each other," she shouted.

Max's hand squeezed hers. She hoped he understood she was only playing it up for her mother's sake.

"And from now on you can keep your flunky security men at home with you because Max happens to be one. He's the one I am entrusting my body to."

"I will have you cut out of any inheritance you might be

thinking is yours if you don't stop speaking to me with such disgrace right this second."

Jordan sighed. It had not been her intention to lambaste her mother, but this time the woman had stepped over the line in sending someone to burglarize her home in the hopes of scaring her straight.

"I'm sorry, Mother, but you've gone too far with this stunt. If you want to disown me, fine. I'm not sure Daddy will be too happy, but fine. I don't want a dime. I want to own my own studio and teach kids to dance. I want to marry the man of my choice and have babies who aren't born thinking money can buy them everything. I want to live my own life and not have you tell me who I should marry for the sake of *your* appearance. I'm going to hang up now, Mother."

She did, pressing the end button on her mother's shriek. Then she powered off the phone.

"Wow."

Jordan sank back into her seat. It took her several seconds to realize she'd pulled to the side of the road and the car sat idling still within sight of Clement's estate. Her cheeks heated at what Max had overheard.

"So shall we just get right to the babies since we've already had unprotected sex or do you think we should get married first?"

Jordan choked on her spit. Max pounded on her back.

"Sheesh. Don't say things like that unless you mean them."

"Who says I don't?"

She stared at the crazy man. "Are you serious?"

"As a heart attack, kamikaze."

She must have looked completely confounded because Max laughed and cupped a hand behind her neck. He urged her closer and kissed the tip of her nose before murmuring to her, "I just have a few stipulations."

"A few?"

"Yep. The bike has to go or you really will give me a heart attack."

"Not a chance, bucko."

He growled against her lips. "You have to let me finance your studio or we'll be old and gray by the time you get it up and running."

"I can think on that one."

"Pole dancing is for my benefit only."

"Hey." She poked him in the ribs, making him grunt. "It's good exercise. And the way we go at it, I'll need all the help I can get."

"And last but not least, seeing as you're so good at it, would you please make a call to my mother too and tell her how it's going to be?"

"Now that I can handle." She melted her lips on his and kissed him until they were both out of breath.

About the Author

Annmarie McKenna lives in Missouri where she stays busy writing, shuffling four kids to various activities and trying to keep sane. She loves to hear from readers and can be reached at annmarmck@yahoo.com. To learn more about Annmarie, please visit www.annmariemckenna.com or join her Yahoo! group for updates on her latest releases or other information http://groups.yahoo.com/group/Annmarie_McKenna.

Hell hath no fury like a scorned woman—with toys.

On His Knees
© 2009 Beth Williamson
Private Lives, Book 1

Renny Johnson has no idea why her ex-husband broke into her house in the middle of the night. She plans to find out—right after he wakes up from a close encounter with his own baseball bat. As long as she's got him tied up, she might as well make him answer every unanswered question about their divorce.

Nicholas sneaked into the house, hoping to retrieve his precious autographed bat without having to face Renny's wrath. He didn't expect her to knock him out with it. Then again, who can blame her? He left her to take a walk on the wild side, to search for that missing something he thought he couldn't find in his marriage.

Now that he's completely at her mercy, he's about to find out how merciless—and how incredibly sexy—his ex can be. The night becomes a wild roller coaster ride of amazing sex, dominance and submission, and maybe the beginning of a brand new chapter in their lives.

Unless the flames burn out of control...

Warning: This title contains a dominant woman, a sexy submissive man, and lots of nekkid, smokin' hot sex.

Available now in ebook from Samhain Publishing.